THAT NIGHT

ALSO, BY DONNA M. ZADUNAJSKY

Novels

Broken Promises

Not Forgotten

The Accident

Books in Series

Family Secrets

Hidden Secrets

Twisted Secrets

Novellas

HELP ME!

Talk To Me

Young Adult

The Dead Girl Under the Bleachers

Buried Secrets

The Body in the Road

THAT NIGHT

Donna M. Zadunajsky

THAT NIGHT

ISBN: —Paperback: 979-8-313959-21-4

ISBN: —Hardcover: 978-1-938037-84-9

ISBN: —eBook: 978-1-938037-83-2

Book Cover Design by: Warrendesign

Interior Format by: Donna M. Zadunajsky

Connect with the Author:

http://www.donnazadunajsky.com

http://www.facebook.com/donnamzadunajsky

http://www.goodreads.com/DonnaMZadunajsky

To all the friends I have made
throughout my life,
THANK YOU

Content Warning

This book contains
depictions self-harm.

Part One

Do you see it?
Through the thickness of the trees.
Through the darkness.
Do you feel it?
It's the very existence of your soul,
leaving your body.

Quoted by: Donna M. Zadunajsky

One

The first day of my senior year arrived, leaving just nine months until graduation. Nine months. It felt like a pregnancy. I had never been pregnant, but I believed school could be as excruciating as giving birth. The teasing and bullying that went on here were relentless. The pressure from teachers and our parents was suffocating.

"Kat, I want so much more for you than I had," my mom once said.

I knew she wanted more for me, but that didn't change how these kids treated each other. School was every kid's worst nightmare, almost like a Freddy Krueger movie—except you don't get killed; you just suffer emotional abuse, sometimes physical.

The school bus jolted to a stop, snapping me out of my daydreaming. Students younger than me were scattered around. Was I the only senior without my own car? Sure, I could drive my father's, but not until six in the evening. I didn't want to think about the car in the garage. The one under the blue tarp. The one I hadn't been in for almost a year. If I were being totally honest, I had nowhere to go or any friends to hang out with anyway.

I sat still while everyone else clambered off the bus. Then, I slid out of the green leather seat and strolled down the aisle. The blazing sun warmed my face as I stepped off the bus and onto the cracked concrete sidewalk. The bus doors swooshed shut behind me, then lurched forward, gears grinding as it drove away. Exhaust fumes hung in the air, drifting up my nose. I coughed, tasting the carbon fumes at the back of my throat. I reached for the water bottle in the side pocket of my backpack when my body rocked backward. For just a split second, my feet left the pavement. I stumbled back, colliding with another kid.

"Sorry," I mumbled as I regained my footing, stepping out of the line of traffic that had formed on the sidewalk. My head whipped around to see who had bumped into me. A boy I hadn't noticed before stopped and glanced over his shoulder back at me.

"Watch where you're going," I shouted.

He smiled at me and gave me a nod.

Completely taken aback, I stood there blinking. A flutter of tingles swirled in my stomach as I admired his muscular build and good looks. I turned, shaking away the images. What was wrong with me? I don't usually gawk at guys, especially ones I don't know.

My chest rose and fell, and a sigh escaped my flesh-colored lips. I rolled my shoulders back, letting them slump beneath my light blue cotton sweater. A semi-warm gust of wind whooshed my auburn hair into my face. I tucked a lock of hair behind my right ear and peered out into the parking lot.

I scanned the scenery. Everyone around me was also staring out into the parking lot. Fewer than half of the students who attended Hoffman High were rooted on the sidewalk, ogling a parked car.

I believed it had nothing to do with the car but with who was sitting inside it. There were rumors about Trevor and Mia breaking up when I returned home from my trip. I was just a little surprised that the rumors were true. Something drastic must have happened for them to split up. I couldn't imagine either of them cheating on the other. So, what tore those two lovebirds apart? I'd have to keep my ears open since I was sure the other students here at Hoffman High would gossip about it.

I shook the thought from my mind and refocused on the car. What I and everyone else saw was not his girlfriend in the passenger seat. At least it didn't look like her. It didn't appear to be a person with blonde hair or even a female. Trevor wasn't gay. Not that being gay was wrong. It was that

Trevor was definitely into girls, or perhaps more accurately, one girl. Mia was the love of his life, and vice versa. I wouldn't be surprised if they got back together.

At that very moment, whispers filled my ears. The same words had echoed through the halls of Hoffman High for years.

"Oh my God, I can't believe it."

"Are you kidding me?"

"Trevor and..."

"I hadn't heard. Did you hear anything?"

"Is he gay?"

"No way! It will destroy Mia."

"No wonder she broke up with him."

And on and on. More gossip. We all stood on the sidewalk, waiting for the person to get out of the car. It reminded me of a movie playing in slow motion, except no one was moving. There was a creak as the car door opened. Trevor Chapman, the all-star football champion, stepped out of the car. He extended his left arm, a gesture I'd seen him do a million times, and ran a hand through his flowing, brown, shoulder-length hair before slamming the car door shut with his right hand. I must admit, he was gorgeous. He acted as if he were in a Gap commercial, the way his shirt clung to his chest and biceps. Let's not forget how his hair cascaded over his shoulders, as if someone were styling it right where he stood. His shirt rose, revealing his muscular abs. Did he feel like a movie star with everyone fawning over him?

I swallowed and glanced down at the ground. I shouldn't be thinking about him like that. Never had I viewed Trevor as a piece of meat. As I scanned the crowd, I noticed that I wasn't the only girl fantasizing about his body. The others, I believed, were struggling to wrap their heads around what the hell was happening.

"Is that Gavin Bowers?" someone asked from the crowd onlookers.

My head whipped back toward the car. My eyes followed Trevor as he glanced to his right. The passenger door opened, and Gavin appeared with a broad smile on his face. He stepped out of the vehicle, soaking in the scene.

I blinked, directing my attention back to Trevor, who wasn't smiling. Nope, today, he was discreet. He didn't make eye contact with anyone, but everyone was watching him. In fact, he stared down at the ground like an obedient dog. Did he sense our eyes on him? If so, he didn't let it show, keeping his emotions sealed like a can of tuna—a skill he had developed after what happened to his father two years ago. But I'll get into that later.

Then again, maybe I acted too soon because now Trevor was smiling. Does that make him a liar? Not necessarily. He had to be the popular, good-looking, all-star football player we imagined him to be. Winning the town its first undefeated state championship last year.

Trevor stepped away from his car and walked toward the school. Gavin slammed the car door and hurried to catch up with him. They had never been friends; I was sure of it. Had I missed this piece of information? I scanned my memory but came up blank. Nope, I didn't recall hearing anything about those two since I'd returned.

Trevor puffed out his chest. He didn't seem to care what anyone thought. To me, it would feel like an itch I couldn't reach in the middle of my back. I didn't like being the center of attention, but he did.

I scanned the scene with curious eyes. Trevor's posture was usually easy to read, but today, I wasn't sure what he was thinking. His demeanor seemed off. God, I hated not knowing. His teammates were going to ask him questions, and he better have a solid explanation. I had to be there when it went down.

With my thumbnail between my teeth—a habit I couldn't seem to break—my mind raced with judgments. I dropped my hand and rested it on the strap of my backpack. Turning away, I hurried up the walk and into the school.

As I walked through the hall lined with lockers, my ears filled with chatter. If it were a competition, the noise inside the school would surely surpass that outside. *But they hadn't witnessed what I had seen.*

The students discussed what they did over the summer and the vacations they took. This town wasn't huge by any means, but that didn't mean everyone knew everyone else's business. Secrets could still be concealed from nosy neighbors who loitered on their front porches. The hushed whispers in the aisles at the local grocery store often revealed more than intended. People in Crawford tried to mind their own business, but they frequently failed miserably.

A week before school started, the administration office sent everyone their class schedule, locker number, and combination. Orientation was optional. Since this is a small school, I already knew most of the teachers and the locations of my classes. Besides, it was always something my mom and I did together.

I stood at my locker, turning my head toward the loud outburst coming from down the hall. Just my luck. My locker was in the same hallway as the dumb, loud jocks. They think they're so much better than everyone else and have no respect for those around them. I watched as a couple of jocks playfully pushed each other around. But two people stood out from that crowd: Gavin and Trevor.

Closing my locker door, I leaned against it and took in the scene. Yes, I'm curious when it comes to unexpected events, like Trevor allowing Gavin to hang out with him and his football buddies. Sometimes, I found myself in situations that were hard to escape. But I liked the detective side of me. I inherited that from my father, who was the detective here in Crawford. I enjoyed searching for clues and uncovering the truth. This summer, however, I promised myself I would mind my own business. The thing was, summer was over.

Gavin was considered a loser at this school. Normally, I didn't label people, but Gavin was different. I genuinely believed he enjoyed being picked on. In fact, some guys from the team had bullied him for years. Did that make him uncomfortable standing there with them, wondering if the jocks were going to stuff him into a locker like they had done last year and the year before? Or maybe he felt like the King of England next to Trevor. Could that be why he was hanging around Trevor? Was Trevor protecting Gavin? No, that didn't seem likely. Trevor wouldn't jeopardize his reputation for someone like Gavin. Would he?

I searched my mind but came up empty. Nothing made sense about Trevor and Gavin being friends. Then again, did something happen over the summer that brought them together? No, that couldn't be true. Trevor wouldn't be caught dead hanging out with Gavin, yet here he was. So, what could it be? How did this happen? Why did it happen? I had to find out. I couldn't just watch like everyone else.

There goes my resolve to not meddle in anyone's life.

I pushed away from the locker and walked down the hall, stopping several feet from where the football team stood. I feigned reading something on the bulletin board.

"What's with the cockroach following you today?" Andrew asked.

I always saw Andrew as Trevor's bitch. He trailed after him and wanted to mimic him. I looked around the scene. Trevor shifted his gaze from his friends to Gavin and then back to Andrew.

"Guys, you all know Gavin Bowers?" Trevor announced.

"Well, duh," Chad replied. "Who doesn't know this douchebag?"

Chad was a defensive lineman. His nickname was The Fridge. If you stepped in front of him on the field, you were going down, and it was going to hurt.

"I want you to be nice to him. He'll be hanging around with us from now on," Trevor announced.

My jaw dropped, and my eyes widened. I didn't see this coming at all. *Hang out with them? What the heck!*

"You can't be serious?" Andrew spat.

"Yes, I am! So, get used to it," Trevor snarled, meeting Andrew's gaze.

Like outside, I could tell Trevor was hiding something.

A secret. I hated secrets. But I loved uncovering the secret. Something was definitely going on.

Andrew stiffened and glanced away like a shy child. Was he terrified of Trevor? Then again, who here wasn't? Trevor sauntered off with his tail between his legs, while Gavin followed one step behind him like a lovesick puppy. He must have a moral reason for letting Gavin stay around him, right?

TWO

I slipped in behind them and followed until Trevor stopped outside one of the classrooms. He muttered something to Gavin, but I couldn't hear what he said. Then he turned and strolled into the classroom. I wanted to feel sorry for him, but I whisked that thought away like a mosquito buzzing around my ear. If you asked me, Trevor deserved whatever happened to him. If he got himself into trouble, then this was his punishment.

I scurried across the hall and into the restroom, ducking into one of the stalls. I flushed and turned to leave the small cubicle when the restroom door swung open. I wasn't sure why I hesitated to leave, but something held me back. Instead, I peered through the narrow gap to see who it was before stepping out of the stall. I didn't know exactly why. I wasn't afraid of anyone. I wasn't being bullied. My stomach churned with uneasiness; the kind you feel right before something bad happens.

This was turning into an interesting day after all. I couldn't believe what I was seeing. A wide smile spread across my face. First, I heard the words exchanged between Trevor and the football team. Second, as I perched behind a locked stall door, Mia Barnes breezed in and stood at the sink.

What were the odds that Trevor's ex-girlfriend would walk into the same restroom I was in? One in seven, to be precise, since there were only seven restrooms in the entire school.

Squinting, I peeked back through the narrow opening as Mia applied lipstick to her lips. The dull fluorescent lights hanging from the ceiling cast a yellowish glow. I couldn't tell which shade she was using, but I hoped it was darker than her pale complexion reflected in the mirror.

My eyes traced over her hair, which had once been long and beautiful but now appeared dry and split like straw. Had a vampire bitten her? Then again, I had been reading too many supernatural books lately. There was no such thing!

The sweater Mia wore draped over her shoulders like a shawl, concealing her thin figure. Perhaps it was so no one would notice how much weight she'd lost in such a short time. Was she on a diet? I don't remember Mia ever being overweight. Was that the reason she and Trevor broke up? There haven't been any other rumors about her since I returned home, aside from the one about her and Trevor ending their relationship. I suppose Mia was the only one who knew the truth behind why she stopped eating. Besides, you can't always trust what people say around here. A story can become all twisted like the roots of a banyan tree, especially with people adding their own perspectives.

But I do recall hearing an argument last night while walking the dog. It came from inside Mia's house. *"I need some normalcy, and school will help instead of being trapped in this house with the two of you,"* Mia hollered.

Why would she need to beg her parents to go to school? Most kids would be thrilled to stay home, though most parents wouldn't want their kids skipping school. They seemed worried about her. Mr. and Mrs. B, as I like to call them, had been strict with Mia her whole life. Ethan, Mia's older brother, usually received all the attention. Did they wonder what had happened to their little girl with the sea-blue eyes? What had caused her to stop eating? Though the real question should be, *why* had she done it? She was one of the thinnest girls at our school, in addition to being popular and smart.

I remember when we used to challenge each other. She almost always won, but it was close most of the time. There are days I miss that. I miss her. Kat and Mia. Mia and Kat. The dynamic duo when we were in middle school, but we weren't in middle school anymore. And we weren't Kat and Mia, Mia and Kat, any longer. We weren't friends anymore.

My back stiffened in attention. Mia dropped the lipstick back into a small black bag and slipped it into the side pocket of her backpack, all while keeping her eyes on the mirror in front of her and occasionally glancing at the stalls behind her. I wondered for a moment if she sensed someone hiding behind one of the closed doors. She showed no sign or urge to look.

Mia let out a weary sigh, allowing her shoulders to slump with fatigue. I bet she wished she were anywhere but here. She had once been a cheerful person—full of life and ambition. Her laughter lingered long after it was heard. She turned and walked toward the exit, pausing for a moment before reaching for the door handle. The small room filled with chatter as the door opened. Mia adjusted the backpack on her shoulder, and a single piece of paper fluttered to the floor. The folded note slipped from the open zipper pocket of Mia's backpack.

Once the door closed, the room fell silent. I quickly unlocked the stall door, dashed to the piece of paper, and picked it up. Mia's name was scribbled on the outside of the note. My fingers searched for the edge of the paper to open it when the restroom door swung open. My heart raced in my chest, pounding against my ribs. I quickly cupped the paper in my hand and shoved it into the back pocket of my jeans, then hurried to the sink to wash my hands. I glanced over my shoulder and noticed two girls from the cheerleading squad. Their laughter stopped the moment they saw me standing there. The sound of running water filled the awkwardness in the air. I hadn't meant to stare at them.

"What are you looking at?" asked the brunette with a look of disgust.

I wanted to say, *"I don't know; I'm trying to figure that out."* Unless you're egging for a punishment, you never sass a cheerleader. They were friends with all the jocks if you catch my drift. So, I turned away, finished washing my hands, dried them, and left the restroom without saying a word.

Once in the hall, my right hand slipped into the back pocket of my jeans. I felt the thick-papered square. I wanted to find a place to hide and read it, but another part of me wanted to return the note to Mia, who was walking down the hallway in the opposite direction. Kids turned as she passed by. Could she sense their eyes on her? Hear the gasps and whispers filling the air and seeping into her ears? If she did, she didn't show any reaction.

I shifted my gaze to the classroom in front of me, strolled across the hall, and entered through the open door. Trevor was seated at a desk in the third row, his neck resting on the metal backrest, and his eyes closed. My cheeks lifted as a smile broke uncontrollably across my face. I hurried past him and took a seat two diagonal spots away from him.

Minutes later, I pulled my gaze away from my cell phone. Mia stood next to Trevor, stiff as a board. His chest expanded as he inhaled deeply. His eyebrows twitched as if he had just tasted the most delicious food. A smile spread across his face. Could he smell her presence there? Smell the sweet fragrance of her perfume lingering in the air? His eyes shot open, and he sat up straight. They locked eyes. The smile vanished from his face, and his mouth fell open.

"Mia, what happened to you?" Trevor whispered.

He sounded like he was about to cry. Had he not seen her in the weeks leading up to school? Why had they broken up? I lived across the street from Mia and had watched from behind the curtain of my bedroom window each time Trevor came to visit her. Then, I remembered her parents had not allowed him inside their house two weeks prior. There was shouting, and then Trevor sauntered down the sidewalk. He climbed back into his car and drove away. Obviously, I didn't know what was happening or what had happened, but it had me thinking. Did they think he did something to her? I was sure he wasn't the cause of whatever was going on between them, but I couldn't be certain. I had been gone all summer.

I knew they were in love. There was no way he would ever hurt her. Would he?

Mia rushed past him and took a seat at the back of the room. She dropped her backpack on the floor against the leg of the chair and rested her head on her arm across the desk. People were staring at her, whispering about her. What secret was she hiding? My chest ached. Even though I shouldn't care, I did. A small part of me wished we were still friends; then I could help her through whatever this was, but that bridge had burned long ago.

Three

Trevor jumped up from his seat and dashed out the door the instant the bell rang. It felt strange; I thought he would want to talk to Mia after everything that had happened between them. He had spent most of the class glancing back at her. What could be more important than Mia? What was he hiding? I needed to find out.

I dashed from my seat and followed Trevor down the hall, weaving through the crowd of students. My body slammed into someone's chest, making me stumble backward and bump into another student. This was shaping up to be a tough day.

"Sorry," I murmured.

Arching my neck, I glanced up at the tall person before me. It was the same boy who had bumped into me outside. *Great*. I peered around him as Trevor disappeared around the corner. I groaned, looking back up at the boy. The more I examined his features, the more he resembled a man rather than a boy. He seemed too old to be attending this school, but most kids these days looked older than their age.

"Excuse me," I growled, positioning my feet in flight mode.

The guy stared at me for a long moment before stepping aside. There was something in his eyes and the way he held himself that sent a shiver down my spine. I didn't know him; I hadn't seen him at school before today. Was he a new kid? He wasn't carrying a backpack or any books. Maybe I shouldn't have snapped at him like that. Being the new kid in a new school is tough and stressful. But I wasn't about to stand here and apologize or be his friend; besides, he was the one who stepped in front of me, not the other way around. I had things to do, like finding out what was going on with Trevor.

I dashed away, my hair blowing behind me as I raced down the hall, leaving the guy in my dust. My stomach soured as I felt him watching me. I didn't have time to waste checking if he was. Speeding down the hall, I turned the corner where Trevor had gone, but he was nowhere in sight.

"Damn it!" I muttered under my breath. I had lost him. I was about to turn away when I spotted Paige Ziel, the Class President, talking to Jim Covinski, my ex-boyfriend.

My mouth hung open for so long that it felt like it was filled with sand. What the hell? Was he dating her now? He wasn't Paige's type. He was a geek who loved photography—my geek, not anyone else's. But we were no longer together, which was my choice, not his.

The truth is, I never stopped liking him; I just needed some space. That was all. I didn't expect him to find someone else and replace me so quickly. Yes, it had been three months, but when you love someone, you don't give up on them. You try to win them back or at least let them know you're still interested. I guess that's what I get for leaving town over the summer.

Keeping my head down but my eyes fixed on them, I slinked in closer. Yes, it was none of my business, but in a way, it was. When it came to matters of the heart, you had to know. Nothing and no one else mattered.

"Hey, can we go somewhere to talk?" Paige asked.

Jim's eyes widened.

Maybe they aren't together. So why did she want to talk to him?

"Yeah, where do you want to go?" His eyes scanned the crowd of students. I quickly ducked behind The Fridge, who was blocking me. For a brief moment, I wondered if Jim was looking for me. No, I doubted he even cared about me anymore. Any idiot could see he had moved on. Shifting my head, I peeked around The Fridge and watched.

"Follow me," Paige said, twirling around as she walked down the hall. She pushed open a pair of double doors that led into the stairwell.

I hurried in their direction and placed a hand between the frame and the door. On tiptoes, I peeked through the small window in the door. There was no one there. Where had they gone? Glancing over my shoulder, I slipped inside, still holding the door with one hand. I pressed my back against the wall, their voices echoing all around me. They were talking on the other side of the wall. Apparently, they didn't know how to whisper.

"What do you want to talk about?" Jim asked.

"We need to do something. I think *he* knows."

My eyebrows narrowed. *He?*

"Do you think it's a good idea to talk here? I mean, what if someone shows up? What if someone overhears us?"

"Jim, it's just us here. Stop being so paranoid," Paige hissed.

"Like you've never been afraid?"

"Seriously, you're going to complain about that now. Look, we need to come up with a plan that includes Mia and Trevor."

"Mia?" Jim asked, sounding a bit confused. "Why is she involved? She wasn't even there! Besides, can't we handle this without them?"

"No, we need to do this as a team."

"Can't you leave me out of this?"

"No, you're just as much a part of this as I am."

"Okay, fine. Set it up with Mia and Trevor, and I'll meet you there."

I flinched, covering my ear with one hand to dull the sharp sound of paper tearing.

"Here's my number. Text me the details on the place and time. I need to get to class," Jim said.

My heart raced as I slipped back through the open door and dashed away. I glanced over my shoulder, but Jim was nowhere to be seen. Had he taken a different route? It was possible he had a class upstairs and used the stairs.

Stopping in my tracks, I looked around. I was going the wrong way; my class was in the opposite direction. I made a U-turn and hurried down the hall, entering the classroom just as the tardy bell rang. First Trevor and Gavin, then Jim and Paige? Whatever was going on had nothing to do with Mia. None of this made sense.

Four

"Alright, class, please settle down. I understand there's a lot to remember on the first day of school," said the English Literature teacher.

Everyone in front of me jumped, including myself, when Paige burst through the door. She had never been late for anything in her life. Well, she shouldn't have been slumming it with my ex-boyfriend.

"Sorry, I lost track of time," she said as she rushed toward the only available seat, which was diagonal from me. "I had a meeting in the office with the principal."

"Do you have a pass?"

"No, sorry. Principal Brown said it was okay and that I didn't need one," she said, her lips spreading into a broad smile, revealing her pearly whites.

"Fine, take a seat, Miss Ziel," the teacher said as he faced the chalkboard to write.

He accepted her story, but I didn't. She was lying about her whereabouts. The principal, really? Unless something had changed, and Jim was now the principal of the school with his office in the stairwell.

I crossed my arms; the corner of my mouth twitched so violently that I feared my jaw might snap. I wasn't sure if I wanted to yank Paige's perfectly combed ponytail or punch her in the head. Instead, I sat there, letting my eyes bore into the back of her head like a raging bull ready to charge.

A few minutes later, a cell phone chimed, once again disrupting the class. Everyone turned toward Paige, and she stiffened like a startled cat. Throughout all the years I had known Paige, she had consistently checked her phone. I thought of her as a bit of a goody-two-shoes, as if she believed she was better than everyone else. It was about time she made a mistake and got into trouble. In fact, everything about Paige seemed off this morning.

I still couldn't believe she was hitting on Jim. How dare she! It wasn't like Paige, and I were best friends. Hell, we weren't friends at all. But she knew we had dated, so why would she do this to me? I'd have to say something to her. I didn't want to see my ex with her, of all people. Anyone but Paige. Or maybe I didn't want him with anyone but me. I pursed my lips. I wasn't sure why I'd claimed I needed space, and now—now he was going out with Paige. I wasn't certain they were dating, but they were being mysterious about something.

"Sorry," Paige said again. Leaning against the desk leg, she reached into her black Brunello Cucinelli handbag and pulled out her cell phone. The screen lit up as she silenced the phone. She opened her worn literature book and propped it up on her desk to read. I leaned forward in my seat to glimpse the message, thankful for my good eyesight. It was from an unknown number.

> **Unknown number:** My Dearest Paige, you have until the end of the week. Then I want your answer, or I'll tell the entire school what I know. I know you have a lot riding on this year, but how do you think Harvard will react when they find out exactly how you achieved such a high SAT score? I would hate for you not to go to your dream school.

I blinked, processing what the text had conveyed. Did that mean what I thought it did? Paige pressed the phone to her chest and surveyed the room. I looked down at my notebook, pretending to take notes.

I glanced at Paige, who was now facing forward. Her rosy cheeks had vanished, and her skin had turned ashen. She wiped her hand on the side of her high-waisted plaid tweed skirt. I was certain that whoever sent the text was blackmailing her. I needed to find out the identity of the unknown sender.

Paige held the phone out to reread the message, then typed a reply to Trevor.

Wait, what? my mind screamed. Trevor? Since when have she and Trevor been talking? What the hell was happening? What had gone down this summer? My dad had sent me to Florida to visit my grandparents, but when I returned three weeks ago, I found that the town had fallen apart without me.

Paige sent Trevor another text. She kept flipping her phone over to check the screen, but he still hadn't replied. Did she expect him to jump every time she needed something? How close had they become over the summer?

The teacher cleared his throat, and when I looked up, I saw him staring at Paige again. She raised her head and swallowed, casually dropping her phone into her purse.

"Yes, I know it's the first day of school, but we need to get our minds working," the teacher said. "Next time, Miss Ziel, I'll take your phone away."

"I'm sorry, it won't happen again," she said.

"I trust that it won't," the teacher said.

Paige twisted her neck and scanned the room until our eyes met. We stared at each other for a moment before she shifted her gaze back to the book on her desk. I hoped she sensed me watching her. She better keep her guard up around me.

Five

A couple of hours later, it was time for lunch. As I weaved my way through the hall, I hurried toward the cafeteria, pausing in the doorway. Paige was on her phone, which was unusual for her. She wasn't the type of student to text during class; she didn't break the rules. Something felt off. If she had cheated, as the text suggested, then she was—well, she was screwed, wasn't she?

First, Trevor was way too into himself, allowing Gavin to hang around him. Second, I saw Paige and Jim slipping into the corridor, whispering about someon*e* knowing something. I didn't understand what they were discussing or who that person was. Still, the image of those two together would be forever etched in my mind. Then there was Mia and the note I had in my jeans pocket, which I still hadn't read. So, the question remained: what was going on with the five of them?

The cafeteria buzzed with activity like hungry bees making honey. My eyes scanned the room, looking for Jim and Paige. I wasn't sure where Mia and Trevor were; I hadn't seen them since first period this morning. I would need to get a copy of their class schedules to keep track of everyone. I should mind my own business, but since my ex was involved, there was no way I was backing off now.

I scanned the lunchroom. Jim always had his candy-apple-red denim backpack slung over his shoulder. He got it at the start of ninth grade and never left home without it. The backpack was easy to spot in a crowd like this, but I didn't see him anywhere. Then, something caught my eye near the far wall. Something red slipped out the door—the door that led to the football field.

"Excuse me. Pardon me," I said, weaving through the swarm of hungry students. I navigated the large, crowded room, feeling as though I was in a pit at a rock concert, with kids pushing and shoving their way into the lunch line.

Once I reached the door, I pushed hard on the metal bar. The door *clanked* as it unlatched. Wincing, I peered over my shoulder, grateful that the noise in the room was much louder and that no one was paying any attention to me. The school didn't allow students outside on the field during lunch. I'm not sure who created that lame rule.

My hand instinctively shot up to shield my eyes from the bright light piercing through. Spots danced in my vision, and I blinked them away. The figure moved away from me and toward the bleachers—Jim, with his red backpack slung over his left shoulder.

In the distance, two people sat next to each other near the top left corner of the bleachers, clearly visible. If it were me, I'd hide behind the concession stand where no teachers could see me if they looked outside.

Mia and Trevor Chapman, the epitome of popularity, were sitting next to each other. Had they gotten back together already? Even if they had, I really didn't care. What confused me the most was Jim. Why was he meeting with them? He wasn't friends with them too, was he? Why were they even out here? And what were they discussing?

A phone chimed to my left. Paige magically appeared around the corner like a rabbit pulled from a hat. She reached into her very expensive handbag and took out her phone. I slinked back inside, hoping to stay invisible. I left enough space to see what she would do next. Obviously, I didn't know what the text said, but I had an idea of who it was from. Paige headed straight for the bleachers. Apparently, she was invited to their private party. Heat rose from my gut to my face. Jim and Paige together?

No!

I wouldn't allow it, so I had to come up with a plan. I needed to figure out what was going on between the four of them. Looking around, I didn't spot Gavin anywhere. Speaking of which, where was Gavin?

Six

I climbed onto the bus, relieved that school was finally over for the day. In no time, I was getting off at the stop sign near my house.

I stumbled twice on the sidewalk like a drunken sailor as my mind revisited the day's events. All day, I had mulled over the note still in my back pocket, wondering who it was from. It must be from Trevor, but maybe not. Mia was a popular girl, or should I say, she used to be. I found out today that she quit the cheerleading squad and turned herself into a *nobody*. Though it wouldn't last long, she was Mia, after all.

"Kat!" a voice shouted from behind me.

I turned around, taking a step back. It was Mia. *What the hell did she want?* My mind raced through every possible scenario of today's events. Mia couldn't have known I was watching them, could she?

"Kat, stop! I need to talk to you," Mia yelled.

I exhaled, paused, and stood on the sidewalk, wanting nothing more than to turn and run away from her. It had nothing to do with being afraid of Mia. That was something I wasn't. There was nothing Mia could do to hurt me. At least not anymore. We used to be friends—best friends, in fact. And it didn't end well. Besides, it was better not to be friends with her. Look at what she did to herself. Someone like that wasn't someone I should hang out with. Clearly, she had issues in her life, and I didn't need the drama.

There was nothing worse than girl drama. At least, that's what my mom always said about her days in high school and college. Maybe Mia knew I had the note that fell from her backpack? No, I doubted that was true. She would have asked for it back. So, what did she want to talk to me about?

"Hey," Mia said, breathing heavily as she stopped beside me.

I hoped she wasn't about to collapse. Although I could have met her halfway, why should I? I wasn't the one who wanted to talk. I had nothing to say to her.

Mia stepped in front of me, blocking my way.

My attention was drawn behind her as I watched a squirrel scamper up the tree with a nut in its mouth. With two weeks left in August, the sun felt hotter than on most days as summer came to a close. I shifted my weight from one foot to the other, squinting as the sun blazed down on me. Sweat trickled down my neck and along my brow. I wiped my forehead with the back of my hand and then rubbed my hand on my jeans.

Mia stood silently, waiting for me to speak. I hoped she couldn't read my thoughts, and I was genuinely afraid that she might be able to. Then, she stepped back and walked down the sidewalk as if she hadn't planned to stop at all.

"Are you coming?" she called over her shoulder.

I paused for a moment before following her, walking beside her as she spoke again.

"She saw you outside."

Initially, her words confused me; then I nodded. Relief washed over me, glad it wasn't about the note. But how did *she* know it was me from so far away?

"Why are you watching us?"

"How did you know it was me?" I wiped another bead of sweat from my forehead with the back of my hand. Why was I sweating so much?

"Not me. Paige mentioned she saw you at the door following Jim. Didn't you two break up?"

"We did, but..." Why was I telling Mia? It was none of her business what happened between Jim and me. "Actually, what were you, Trevor, Paige, and Jim doing out on the bleachers? You hardly ever hang out with that crowd, or at all?"

Mia paused, turned, and looked at me. "Say it. I know you want to."

"Say what?"

"That you hate me and want nothing to do with me."

"I don't think I need to say the words. You already know."

Mia's expression darkened, a deeper shade than the colorless glow she had worn all day. She leaned in close as if about to share a secret, not wanting anyone else to overhear, even though no one else was around. We were the only two on the sidewalk. "You know what? It's none of your business. So, what if we're all having lunch together?"

"Out on the football field? On the bleachers? Where students aren't allowed during lunch?"

"Yeah, what's wrong with that?" Mia snapped. "We can do whatever we want."

I laughed. "Yes, of course, since you're all so popular and run the whole damn school. Except Jim and Paige were with you. It didn't even look like you were eating lunch, though you could really use the food these days," I snapped, surprising myself. I hadn't meant to say those words. What had come over me? I don't speak badly to anyone. It must be the note in my pocket. Or maybe it was because the four of them were huddled together like they had been friends forever, even though they hadn't. It felt strange. And secretive.

I hated secrets. I hated the drama, which was exactly what was happening between us right now. How did this conversation escalate to the point of us shouting at each other? Was I really envious of her? I didn't know, but I wanted nothing more than to walk away from Mia. I didn't want to get physical with her. God, I didn't want to fight her. Why would I even think we would end up fighting?

Mia fixed her gaze on me, her jaw muscles twitching slightly.

"Go ahead, Mia. Hit me," I said, my pulse racing.

"Hit you?" she questioned. "Why would I hit you? What's wrong with you, Kat?" She gave me a disgusted look.

"Well, to start, you seem upset for some unknown reason. It can't be because I was standing outside watching you all, so what's going on? Are you all in *cahoots* or something?"

The color drained from her face as if she'd seen a ghost. She swallowed hard, then stepped back from me as though I had struck her. Her eyes darted around, searching for anyone who might be listening. I barely caught the words that slipped from her thin, pink lips as she took another step back, turned, and hurried away.

"How did you know?" were the words Mia whispered. What did she mean? I hadn't been close enough to hear their conversation on the bleachers. I had been bullshitting with her, but I had been right. There was definitely something going on between the four of them, and I was certain Gavin was at the center of it all. Now, all I needed to do was figure out what Gavin was holding over their heads.

Minutes later, I arrived home and sat on my bed. My foot jittered on the floor while my right thumb traced the letters, spelling out the name M.I.A.

I bit down on my bottom lip and rolled my shoulders back. It was wrong to snoop around in Mia's business, but if I wanted to learn more about her and what the others were hiding, I needed to read the note. I bit my lip again and unfolded the paper. The words appeared upside down, so I flipped the paper over and read.

Seven

The next morning, as I lay beneath the comfort of my duvet blanket, I couldn't shake the words written on the paper from my mind. I spent hours reading the letter repeatedly.

I rolled over and opened the small drawer of my nightstand, pulling out the sheet of paper, the note from Mia's backpack. As I lay there, I reread the words that weighed heavily in my gut.

Mia,

Do you think killing yourself is a way out? That you can escape me? You'll never get away from me. You're a smart girl. I know I can count on you to keep my secret. Our secret. Do you think you can just end your life because of this? I won't make it that easy for you. I need you. You need me. So, don't think about trying it again!

"Disturbed" wasn't the right word for what I read in that note. Mia had tried to take her own life. How? When? Why?

My mind flicked back to moments in our younger days. Mia loved snacking on Kit Kats and Snickers. We were often in the kitchen making something, especially oatmeal raisin cookies, her favorite. She was always full of happiness and looked radiant, no matter what she wore. Then, the images of Mia in the restroom flashed through my mind. Thin and fragile. I hadn't seen her since the beginning of summer. Now, I wish I had stayed in town. Did Trevor know about her situation? Did the school know? I remembered seeing her get out of a car, carrying a suitcase two days after I got home. Had they sent her away, too? If so, that didn't mean the town was aware of what had happened in her home or what she had done to herself. Did they?

Suicide? I never would have imagined Mia as the type. Were there really types? Look at Gavin. He seemed like the kind of person who would take his own life, with his low self-esteem and the way everyone belittled him. But a popular cheerleader? No one would ever think she would do that.

The words Trevor had spoken echoed in my mind. *"Mia, what happened to you?"* He had no idea, and if he doesn't know what she tried to do, does that mean no one else knew either? But I do.

Whoever wrote the note did something to Mia—something that made her want to end her life. There was no name, so I didn't know who wrote the letter. What could have happened that was so tragic for Mia to take her own life? I didn't believe Gavin was capable of something like this, but I didn't hang out with him. What does this person mean by "*You'll never get away from me*" and "*Our secret*"?

My mind raced back to yesterday when Mia, Trevor, Jim, and Paige were sitting together on the bleachers, which seemed odd to me. How did Jim and Paige fit into all this? They weren't friends. *Or boyfriend and girlfriend,* my mind protested. At least, I hoped not. They had never even hung out together, had they?

Then there was Mia's reaction before she skittered away when I mentioned the word 'cahoots.' Even though I was just joking, Mia seemed to take it as if I knew what had happened, but I didn't. I know nothing. I'm clueless, but I will find out what's going on.

It was in my nature to solve this little mystery involving the four of them and whoever had placed this note in Mia's backpack. I needed to pay close attention to Mia, and I was grateful to live near her so I could observe her every move.

I took a deep breath, letting it out as I flipped the blankets to the side and slipped out of bed. My feet sank into the frieze carpet, feeling its softness against my skin. I had tossed and turned most of the night, my mind stewing over the note to Mia. I wouldn't let her know I had it or that I had read it. Not yet.

I paced the floor of my bedroom, contemplating my next move while chewing on my thumbnail. Should I confront Mia? What would I say if I did? We hadn't been friends in years. But this wasn't about friendship; it was about uncovering what had happened to her. Would Mia actually share why she tried to end her life? I doubted it. It wasn't that simple. Nothing was ever that simple. Mia had her reasons, whether they were selfish or not.

She had lost a substantial amount of weight, which indicated that something had happened, and I wanted to know the truth. I needed to know why Mia did what she did. Yet, in the back of my mind, I realized that Mia wouldn't just come out and tell me.

Second, I needed to return the note to her. Sure, I could tell her the truth—that it had simply fallen out of her backpack and onto the restroom floor yesterday. But I had read it first. Oh, and I had made a copy for myself. All good detectives kept copies as proof, even if I wasn't sure what the note meant.

"Shit," I muttered. What if Mia was searching for the note? Did she even know it existed? I had to find a way to return it to her.

If I put the note on Mia's porch, I'd need to leave the house quickly and hide behind the tree across the street. I had to make sure Mia found the note. After that, I would have to hurry to the bus stop so I wouldn't be late for school, still wishing I had a car.

Of course, I would have to do all this without getting caught, which wouldn't be easy. Mia could spot me as soon as I left the cover of the tree. Alternatively, I could place the note on the porch, run back to my house, and wait for Mia to come out. She would see the note, and I'd leave for school at the same time. Yes, that was my plan.

I opened the bedroom door, and Eva, our Golden Retriever, followed me out.

"Hey, you're up early," my dad said from the kitchen table, where he sat reading the newspaper every morning.

"Yeah, I thought I would get to school a little earlier today."

He folded the paper and faced me. "Oh?"

"It's nothing, Dad. I just want to get there before the other students."

It wasn't a complete lie. I hadn't expected my dad to still be at home this morning. Then, the thought struck me. The bus wouldn't arrive for at least another hour, so how was I going to get to school? If I had to walk, it would take too long. I really hadn't considered this plan thoroughly, and I hoped my dad wouldn't question me about it.

"I wanted to see you this morning before I left. You know, to talk like we always do."

I smiled. Yes, this was true. We talked about things even more now that my mom had passed away.

"Come, sit down. You don't need to rush out of here. Besides, I can drive you to school, so you won't have to walk. According to my watch..." He turned his wrist over to check the time. "The bus won't be picking you up for another forty-five minutes."

Lightness filled my chest. That would be a great idea; I could slip the note into Mia's locker. "Okay, sure." I looked out the open door toward the yard. Eva dashed back to the house and up the steps, brushing against my legs. I shut the door. The dog went straight for her food bowl, expecting me to feed her.

I dumped two scoops of dog food into her bowl and refreshed her water. Then, I pulled out a chair and sat down next to my dad. I grabbed the box of Raisin Bran from the table, poured some into my bowl, and added milk.

"How's school going?"

"Everything is good so far. It's day two, so there isn't much happening."

He let out a low chuckle. "That's a stupid question. Is the school doing any awareness programs since your friend Mia attempted to take her own life?"

I sat frozen like a deer caught in the headlights. *How did he know?* It never crossed my mind that my dad would find out. He was a detective, and we lived right across the street from them. Of course, he knew. "Why didn't you say anything when I got home? You know, about Mia and what she did?" *How long had my father been wanting to say something to me? Does he think I know why she did it?* "When did it happen?"

He cleared his throat. "I was walking the dog and heard screams coming from their house. I ran over there and…" His eyes shifted away from mine. "Mia had slit her wrists."

I choked on the cereal stuck in my throat. I grabbed my dad's coffee cup and guzzled down what was left of his coffee.

"Are you okay, sweetheart?"

I blinked rapidly as I processed the words. *She cut her wrists.*

"I take it she hasn't talked to you about it?"

"We're not friends anymore," I replied, shoving a spoonful of cereal into my mouth. I glanced over at my dad, who stared at me with raised eyebrows and pursed lips. He should know that we weren't friends, right? We hadn't hung out in years.

"Not friends? Since when? You two were so close. It was difficult to separate you both when you were young."

I turned away, not wanting to see the pain in his expression. I finished chewing. "Since the beginning of seventh grade, I chose my own path, and so did she. Right now, grades are my priority. I need them to get into a good college, Dad."

"Not more than friends, I hope. Everyone needs a friend. Maybe you can talk to her. She may need someone to confide in, maybe someone like you who had been a friend.

"Dad!" I shouted. There it was again. Why had I been getting so angry lately? Yesterday, I barked at Mia and today, at my father. His eyes widened, and a stern look emerged. "I'm sorry. I didn't mean to snap. You're asking too many questions. It feels like you're interrogating me."

"Sorry, it's just that… have I been too busy lately to not know these things about you? I don't like that there are secrets between us. I know it's been tough without your mom here," he said, running a hand through his hair. "You know you can talk to me. I want you to talk to me. Are you sleeping any better since you got back home?"

"Dad, it's not you or your work. I've just been busy with my own stuff. Yes, you've been busy too, but Eva and I are fine." I glanced down and stroked Eva's head, then looked back up at my father. "You don't need to worry about me. I'm not suicidal like some kids at my school."

"Are there others?"

My stomach sank. I just wanted the conversation to end. "Don't act so surprised. Weren't you in high school before? Weren't there kids who seemed depressed or who were picked on by the popular kids?"

"Yeah, I guess you're right." He picked up his coffee cup, groaned when he saw it was empty, and then set the cup back down. "But you would talk to me if you were, you know, depressed?"

I sighed. "Yes, Dad. I would let you know if I were feeling depressed. Can we talk about something else before we have to leave? Do you have any interesting cases you've been working on?"

"Well, there's nothing I can share with you since it's confidential," he grinned.

I stopped listening and narrowed my eyes at the newspaper article lying in front of my dad. I reached out and slid the top section toward me.

"They haven't released a name yet."

The hairs on the back of my neck stood straight up like icicles hanging from a tree branch. I didn't need to look to know my dad was watching me. Was he waiting for a reaction? If so, I didn't have one. I didn't know the person in the paper.

"It's a shame how they found that girl out in those woods," he said, shifting in his chair. "Stabbed several times, they say. No weapon was found near the scene, either. So far, there are no witnesses or suspects." He coughed into his hand.

I listened to my father as he spoke. The only thing he forgot to mention was where they found the girl's body.

Eight

The article mentioned they found the girl in the woods near Camp Wilson, the same camp Trevor attended for the past four years. Did any of the others go to this camp as well? It seemed unlikely Paige did. She wasn't exactly the outdoorsy type, if you know what I mean, with her pleated skirts and Louis Vuitton purses. Besides, I just couldn't picture her camping and swimming in the lake.

Jim, on the other hand, loved fishing and hunting, but he had never mentioned that he'd attended a summer camp. Maybe he didn't feel comfortable telling me, thinking I'd make fun of him, which I wouldn't. It was also possible his parents pushed him out of the house. I was sure Mia wasn't there. Though, it could be a reason to kill yourself if you had done something unthinkable. Like killing a person.

I shook my head at the notion, but it didn't explain the note. It felt more... *personal*. Of course, it could just be coincidental that it was the same camp where they found the dead girl. But this changed everything, and I would need to ask questions. However, asking questions could raise a red flag. Then they would know I was aware of something. Yet, I didn't know if any of them had done anything at all. I was speculating, but every good detective had to start somewhere. I'd need to come up with a plan and figure out how to find my answers.

My mind whirled again like a tornado, wondering what happened that night and who killed that girl. Why was I assuming Trevor had anything to do with her? Or Jim and Paige? Though Paige and Jim acted very cagey in the stairwell yesterday. They were talking about a *"he"* knowing something, but who was *he*? Had they gone to that camp and stumbled upon her in the woods? But if they did, why didn't they just call for help? And that still doesn't explain who *he* was. These were all important questions I needed to find answers to.

"Hey." My dad snapped his fingers in front of my face. "Are you in there? You're spacing out again."

"Uh, yeah, I'm here," I replied, coughing into my hand. I grabbed the orange juice in front of me, poured some into a glass, and gulped it down; then I poured myself some more.

"Are you certain you're, okay?"

I stopped drinking and placed the empty glass down on the table. "Breathe," *I told myself. "Just breathe."* I didn't want to have one of my panic attacks in front of him. He had never seen me have one, and he'd probably freak out. I closed my eyes, took another deep breath, and then opened them. We stared at one another.

"It's really sad, you know," I nodded toward the newspaper. "That the girl was killed so close to where we live. It's a tragedy."

"I agree." He paused for a moment, then scooted his chair back from the table and stood up. "Wrap it up; we're leaving in a few minutes."

Just like that, the conversation ended.

~

Once at school, I went straight to Mia's locker. I glanced around; the hallway was empty. I slipped the folded note into the slot and listened as it thudded to the floor of the locker before walking away. I had plenty of time to compose myself before class. I hurried down the hall toward the library, trying to figure out how I could keep an eye on the four of them without raising suspicion. I took out my notebook and began jotting everything down, including questions I needed to ask, then headed to the office. I used to volunteer my time assisting in the front office with filing and some computer work for the ladies, which made it easy to obtain a copy of Trevor, Mia, Paige, and Jim's class schedule. It didn't occur to me until I was halfway to my class that I should have gotten a copy of Gavin's, but these four will suffice for now. They would eventually lead me to him anyway. I was sure of that.

Andrew's booming voice caught my attention, halting me in my tracks. I stood off to the side, feigning interest in my book.

"Why is this dweeb hanging around us?" Andrew asked, extending an arm and pushing Gavin to the floor.

"What the hell!" Trevor shouted as he helped Gavin to his feet.

"This is bullshit. You being friends with this jerk," Andrew huffed. "I'm outta here." Andrew stomped away.

Trevor averted his gaze from Andrew. "So, are you guys ready for practice this evening after school?"

Several of them replied with a head bob instead of verbally responding. Maybe they were afraid of getting their heads cut off by Trevor.

"Great, I'm glad we're on the same page," Trevor said, turning to walk away.

I ambled away and slipped down another hallway—the same one where Mia's locker was located. The hall was empty. Where was everyone? A door to my right began to close. I glanced up at the ceiling, where a large clock hung. Shit, I was going to be late for class. I turned and hurried back down the hall. The second bell rang just as I dashed through the open door of my Calculus class.

No heads turned my way as I raced down the row and took my seat near the back. I glanced over at Mia. She had her textbook propped open on her desk and was reading something. Something that looked awfully familiar. It was the note I had placed in her locker that morning. Her face turned as white as cotton. She turned her head. I didn't have time to look away. Our eyes locked. What was she thinking? Did she think I had left the note? I did, but I didn't write it. My eyes diverted to her hand holding the note. She was trembling.

She knew.

Mia knew who had written the letter, and she felt scared.

Nine

I should stop, but I can't walk away now. I need to know the truth—the whole truth of what happened at camp and to Mia. I'm about to enter potentially dangerous territory. I shouldn't care about her, but now that I've read the note, I'm more curious than ever about what happened to her. Why did she contemplate suicide as a way out? Or did she do it for attention? Something Mia was good at achieving, but I was sure this was something much deeper. The way she studied me with those sea-blue eyes revealed that something terrible made her do what she did.

First, I'd start with the girl who was stabbed to death in the woods. That was also the same camp that Trevor and possibly Jim went to. I didn't know about Paige. As I mentioned before, she didn't seem like the type to attend some outdoor camp. Still, could it all just be a coincidence? It doesn't matter. Something happened this summer because they're all running around and hiding behind closed doors.

The images of what might have happened swirled in my mind as if I were on a boat rocking back and forth. The girl in the article—I had never seen her before this morning. She didn't attend our school; I was certain of it. I wanted to uncover the truth about how she died. They were hiding something, and I was determined to find out what it was and what really occurred that night. What was the connection between that girl and the four of them? Unless there was no connection at all, which I had already considered, and it could all just be one big coincidence. I decided I had to talk to him. There was no way around it.

~

At lunch, I grabbed an apple from the bowl in the cafeteria and made my way back through the halls. I stopped outside the theater room, a place Jim liked to go to be alone. It was also a spot where we had sat and had lunch together a few times. I had checked the cafeteria first, but he wasn't there, so this was the only other place I hoped he'd be. Unless he was with them, but I didn't think so. I had noticed Paige talking to another girl on my way here.

I peeled the heavy door open and slowly closed it, not wanting to reveal my presence if he were here. I wanted to catch him off guard, though I wasn't sure what I would find him doing. Would he be happy that I came? I hoped so. I missed him but didn't know how to express that. Or was I simply fueled by jealousy at seeing him with Paige? I don't know. I can't distinguish between the two. Love was tricky like that.

I strolled down the aisle, flanked by rows of upholstered chairs on either side. The school theater resembled the seating at a movie theater. I had sat in these seats many times for school plays and chorus performances, a tradition my mom embraced even though I wasn't the one on stage. My heart ached as I realized it had been four months since she passed away.

Pancreatic cancer took her life shortly after the doctors diagnosed her. I watched her change from a radiant, beautiful woman into a cancer patient. She lost a significant amount of weight during the first month of chemotherapy and radiation—an image that will forever be embedded in my memory. But what hurt the most was the fact that I would never see her again. I would never talk to her or laugh at the silly things she said and did. I missed her so much, and my father did, too, even though he thought he was good at hiding it from me. I know he was only trying to be strong around me, but it was different for him. He wasn't my mom. I couldn't talk about things with my dad the way I could with her.

I didn't have time to prepare for what was about to happen. Not that I could've stopped my mom from dying and shattering both my heart and my life. I shut myself off from the world, angry at God for letting her die. Didn't He know I needed her here? I needed someone to talk to when things got tough, and I didn't know how to fix them. Was that why I broke up with Jim?

A light flickered above the stage as I climbed the few steps and then stopped. I turned and gazed around the room, something I hadn't done when I came here with him. I had always wanted to know what it looked like from up here—to see the audience from the stage and feel the adrenaline pulsing through my veins. The ultimate thrill of people watching you perform on stage. It's daunting if you're not someone comfortable performing in front of others like I am.

"What are you doing here?"

I whipped around but saw no one. The curtains shifted, and he emerged from the shadows. My stomach warmed with small flutters of excitement—or was it fear? "I…" My words faltered.

"You what?" Jim asked.

"I, um, wanted to speak with you."

"About?"

His nostrils flared. I'm not surprised he was upset with me. I had broken up with him. I shattered his heart, and the sad part was I did it when I needed him the most. The day after my mom's funeral, I broke it off with him. I hadn't returned to school, even though there were only a few days left. The teachers allowed me to take my finals online. Then, my dad sent me off to Florida. I didn't give Jim any explanation for why I ended it, and I did it through a text message, of all things. I was a coward and felt ashamed of what I had done and how I ended things.

"Never mind, it was a mistake to come here." I turned to leave. The apple I had eaten threatened to come back up. Why was this so difficult for me? I should pretend he was someone else and ask him what I wanted to know, then leave. But he wasn't someone else; he was the love of my life.

"No, wait!" His voice echoed around me like a speaker.

I stopped at the top of the stairs, waiting and listening, but I didn't turn around. My breath burst in and out as I contemplated what to do, and my heart palpitated hard and fast.

"Kat, can we talk?"

Electric tingles flowed through my body once again. I missed the way he said my name. Did he miss me too? He wanted to discuss our break-up, which wasn't what I had come to talk to him about. I turned back around, looking straight at him. God, I missed him. I longed to feel his arms around me. *Stop!* I fumed inside. I wasn't here to get back together with him or talk about us at all. That was something I wanted to put off for another time. Like never. Though there would never be a right time to talk about what I had done to him. To us.

"Pl…," he paused. "Please, talk to me."

He never begged, especially with me.

For me.

Because of me.

He stepped closer.

The exotic, smooth scent of his body wash enveloped me. I swallowed, longing to feel the warmth of his touch against my skin—to hold him close and have him love me again.

He stepped closer to me.

Be strong and just ask him, my inner voice urged. I was ready to chicken out and run away, but I wasn't one to shy away from challenges. "Are you and…" I paused, standing tall and lifting my chin higher before speaking. "Are you and Paige a couple?" I finally asked, even though it wasn't really what I wanted to know. *You're such a coward, Kat.*

His brows furrowed. "You're kidding me, right? Me and Paige?" He huffed, his face reddening. "Is that why you're here? Do you want to know if I'm dating someone else? Dating Paige? A girl I don't want to be with. A girl I have nothing in common with. A girl who isn't you?"

My mouth fell open. Did that mean he still wanted me? All I had to do was ask for forgiveness, and he would wrap me in his long, slender arms and hold me tight. Then, I would never hurt again. No, I didn't believe it was that simple. Love wasn't simple. Love was complicated. He should never forgive me for breaking up with him, especially not after the way I had ended things.

"Come on, Kat. Don't you understand? You're everything I ever wanted. You're everything I want right now."

My heart galloped beneath my black cardigan like a thoroughbred. Tell him *you miss him too, my mind urged. Apologize for everything.* But I couldn't. That wasn't why I was here.

"Kat?"

"I..." Just ask him, and it'll all be over. Then, you can run away and never be happy again. I closed my eyes, inhaling and then exhaling. "I came here to ask if you were at Camp Wilson this summer?"

His eyes shifted down to the floor and back up to me as his shoulders slumped. "Yeah, my dad said it would be a fun experience for me to get me out of the house for a change," he replied. "Not just sitting around playing video games all summer."

He was telling the truth. His eyes narrowed to meet mine. "Oh, and how was camp?" *Nice.*

He scratched the back of his neck while looking down at his feet again. The bell rang, and he straightened up. “I have to get to class,” he muttered, turning and slipping behind the curtain.

Saved by the bell. I stared at the empty spot where he had stood. He had been there. That meant he knew about the dead girl in the woods, right? Now, I needed to figure out what my next move should be. He hadn’t admitted anything to me, but he didn’t need to; his actions spoke volumes about what I needed to know.

Ten

I stood by my locker, putting the new textbooks inside. I had never wanted a day to end as much as I did today. But there were still two more classes to get through before I could go home and hide away from the world.

The awkward conversation I had with Jim lingered at the forefront of my mind. There was no way he would talk to me again. Why would he? I sought him out not to discuss our breakup but to ask if he went to Camp Wilson this summer. And let's not forget that I wanted to know if *he* and *she* were dating. I'm such an idiot. I could have made everything right again. My heart was whole, but I threw it all away for what—some dead girl I didn't even know.

I banged my head against the locker door, then rested it there as my mind replayed the scene over and over like a merry-go-round. Spinning in circles. Around and around. Why was it so hard to talk to him? It hadn't been hard while we were dating, but now I couldn't even look at him. Was it because of how I had ended it? Well, duh? What I did was unthinkable, unforgivable. I wouldn't blame him if he never wanted to speak to me again.

My body stiffened, cringing at the shrillness of *her* voice ringing in my ears like fireworks on the Fourth of July. God, why did Paige have to be so loud? I turned my head to the right. She stood several lockers down from me, and she wasn't alone. I quickly fumbled for the handle on my locker, grateful I hadn't spun the combination of the lock, and hid behind my locker door, listening.

"So, have you thought about it much?" Gavin asked.

"I won't be your fake girlfriend or any type of girlfriend, so back the hell off," Paige spat in a low whisper.

"Okay, okay." He raised his hands in front of him as if to ward her off like a rabid animal. "But you better agree to something, Paige, or else I'm going to the police," he warned, poking a finger into her chest.

Paige recoiled from his touch.

Police? What would Gavin have on her to go to the police about? Better yet, what did perfect Paige do that had Gavin blackmailing her? I shut the locker door just as he hurried past me. His eyes scanned me from head to toe. Was he really checking me out? Gross.

Paige turned, and our eyes met. Her skin flushed. She staggered away and hurried down the hall in the opposite direction. *Interesting.* Now, all I had to do was figure out what he held over Paige's head.

My mind flicked back to yesterday when Paige received the text in class. If I remember correctly, the text said that Paige had better do what he wanted, or the school would find out how she got such high SAT scores.

Wait!

He said he would go to the police. If she cheated on the test, he would report it to the school, not the police. So, what else did he know that would lead him to go to the police instead of the school?

Eleven

The last bell rang, signaling the end of another school day. I exhaled deeply as the stress of the day melted away. If I had to do it all over again, I wouldn't have gone to see Jim at lunch. There was no pat on the back for a job well done; instead, I was kicking myself for my mistake. *Great job, Kat. You really know how to make a guy hate you.*

Desks scraped across the floor as the rambunctious students raced from their seats and into the hall, excited to go home, just like I was. The moment I entered the hall, I was absorbed by the crowd of students, like rush hour in New York City.

I navigated through the crowded hall toward the school exit, relieved I didn't have to stop at my locker. Once outside, I took a deep breath of fresh air, savoring the sweet, crisp scent of autumn approaching. Ohio changes its weather like a teenage girl choosing an outfit for a date; you never know what the temperature will be.

I scanned the parking lot for Trevor and his little crew, but they were nowhere to be found. In fact, Trevor's car was absent from its usual spot. Had he left? According to the conversation with his jock friends earlier, he had practice after school. But if he had practice, then where could he be?

The weather was pleasant, so I decided to walk home instead of taking the bus. I needed time to myself to think about how I would uncover what Trevor, Mia, Paige, and Jim were all up to. Even though my detective instincts pointed toward Gavin.

"Hey, Kat. You got a sec?"

Someone shouted my name. I turned around to see Gavin jogging toward me. *Speak of the devil*. I continued walking, hoping he'd take the hint and leave me alone. It wasn't that I hated him; he was just a nuisance to me and everyone around him. Maybe that was why the jocks liked to pick on him—he was an easy target.

"Hey, wait up! Why are you walking away from me?" he shouted.

I halted and turned around. "What do you want, Gavin? The last time I checked, we didn't hang out. We're not friends."

"Thanks for caring so much. I never thought of you as a bitch until now."

I stepped back as if he had splashed ice-cold water in my face. "What did you call me?"

"You heard me. I can't believe you would do that to him."

My eyes darted from side-to-side as I searched my mind. What was he talking about? Then it hit me.

"He and I might not be friends anymore because of you, but what you did was really mean and foolish, Kat."

"Thanks to me? I had nothing to do with Jim not wanting to be friends with you anymore. You messed that up on your own. As for Jim and my relationship," I said, not feeling the need to explain myself to him. "I'm sorry for what I did to him, but this is none of your business. What happens between Jim and me is between us. It doesn't involve you." I stood tall, my chest puffed out.

"Well…"

"Well, what, Gavin?!" my voice rose. "This doesn't concern you, so leave me alone." I rushed down the sidewalk, hoping he wouldn't follow me. Anger bubbled inside me. Gavin had no right to talk to me like that. As if what he did to Jim was acceptable. *Screw him.*

My feet slapped against the sidewalk as I turned the corner onto Franklin Street, moving at a fast pace. From the corner of my eye, I hadn't expected to see Gavin's black Buick LeSabre driving slowly past me. How did he get out of the parking lot so fast? I glanced his way. He stared at me through the passenger window.

“Keep driving,” I muttered.

As I walked home, I had a spooky intuition that someone was following me, watching me. I kept glancing over my shoulder, scanning the scenery, but I didn’t see anyone. There were no cars with people in them or anyone walking behind me, at least none that I could spot. There was no one else out here but me; still, I couldn’t shake the feeling. I quickened my pace as the knot in my stomach tightened.

With adrenaline pumping through my veins, I arrived home twenty minutes later. I wanted nothing more than to be inside, locked away from the world. *He called me a bitch.* I laughed out loud. Wow! Gavin had some nerve after what he did to his best friend.

Jim told me why he and Gavin were no longer friends. Eight months ago, Gavin had confided in Jim that he disliked Jim wanting other things, like dating me. Gavin expressed feeling alone because no girl ever considered him as a potential boyfriend. So, Gavin went on Snapchat and fabricated a story about Jim fondling him and wanting to engage in sexual acts with him, claiming that Jim was gay. This led Jim to end their sixteen-year friendship. I hadn’t seen the post since I don’t have an account, but the gossip in the school hallways eventually reached me before Jim could explain what Gavin had done.

Once inside the house, I locked the front door and headed toward the kitchen. When I entered the room, Eva jumped up on all fours.

"Hey, you! Do you want to go outside?"

The dog wagged her tail, dancing all the way to the backdoor. I reached out and unlocked the door. Eva rushed outside just as my cell phone chimed. I reached into the side pocket of my backpack and pulled it out. It was a text message from an unknown number. My mind flicked back to yesterday. Paige had received a text from an unknown number. Could it be the same person? If so, why were they sending me a text? I wasn't part of the Trevor gang. I had nothing to do with whatever they were up to. Well, of course, I had to open the iMessage. I needed to know what this person wanted from me. In the back of my mind, I wondered if it was Gavin.

Eva barked, startling me. With one hand on my heart, I reached back with the other and opened the door. Eva bounded inside, nearly knocking me over.

"Settle down, girl," I said to the dog. I walked over to the jar by the fridge, grabbed a couple of dog cookies, and gave them to her. Then, I headed down the hall toward my bedroom. My phone chimed again; this time, it was a message from my dad. I swiped up and read the text.

> **Dad:** I'll be home late. There's some money in the top drawer of the kitchen. Please order pizza. Love you.
> **Me:** Okay. Love you too.

With my arm outstretched, ready to toss my cell phone on the bed, my eyes caught sight of the one at the top left—the message from the unknown. I tapped the icon, which showed two text messages: one from my dad, which I read, and the other from the unknown, which was still black and bold. My finger hovered over the unread message, hesitating. What could the unknown want from me? Better yet, what do they have on me?

"Open the message, Kat," I said to the room. Eva's head lifted from the bed, looking at me with a quizzical expression. "What? You know I talk to myself all the time." Eva laid her head back down on the bed, letting out a snort as if she understood everything I had said.

I closed my eyes, inhaled, then exhaled and tapped on the message.

Twelve

> **Unknown:** Mind your own business, Kat. I would hate for something to happen to you while you're walking home all alone. What happened has nothing to do with you. Your daddy won't be able to save you this time. Walk away now before it's too late.

I read and reread the message. What did the unknown person mean by, *"Your daddy won't be able to save you this time"*? I wasn't sure what they were talking about. When had my dad ever saved me? *"What happened has nothing to do with you."* Were they referring to the girl in the woods? Yes, of course, because I had asked Jim questions, and he probably went and told the others. Was this some kind of joke? Were they trying to scare me because I wanted to know the truth? The truth that they were all hiding.

I paced back and forth from the bed to the door, but nothing became clear to me. I couldn't figure out what this person was talking about or who they could be. I was certain it wasn't Jim or Mia; their contact information was saved on my phone. That just left Trevor, Paige, or Gavin. What were they afraid I was going to uncover? Had one of them killed that girl? And if so, why?

~

Much later that night, I jumped awake. The floorboard creaked outside my bedroom door. Eva lifted her head and then lay back down, letting out a heavy grunt. I listened as whoever was on the other side of the door stopped and then headed down the hall away from my parent's room. I let my head fall onto the pillow. It was my dad coming home from work. I glanced at the clock next to the bed. It was almost midnight. Was he just now going to bed? He must have been working on the recent case about the girl in the woods.

Light crept under the door, followed by the squeak of the cabinet door opening. A plate being removed echoed through the wall on the other side of my room. I threw the blankets off me and climbed out of bed. Slipping my feet into my slippers, I padded to the door and stepped into the hall. A *ding* sounded from somewhere in the house, but I couldn't tell where. It didn't sound like the microwave; it was more like a doorbell chime. I stood in the kitchen's open doorway, watching my dad toss several slices of pizza onto a plate before placing it in the microwave.

"You're up late," I said.

My dad spun around. "Jesus, Katherine. What did I say about sneaking up on people?"

"Sorry, Dad." My dad rarely scared easily, which indicated he was tense about something. The case? I wasn't sure.

"Did I wake you?"

I shook my head. I had already been awake, my brain rehashing everything that had happened lately. "Why are you getting home so late?"

"It's true, but I've actually been home for a while now." He slipped his hand into the front pocket of his pants, pulled out his cell phone, and glanced at it before placing it face-down on the counter.

"Any updates?"

He shook his head. "Nothing yet, and I can't tell you if we do," he said with a half-smile.

"It's always worth a shot."

He walked over to me and gave me a hug, saying, "Go back to sleep. You look exhausted."

I nodded and yawned, more than he realized. "Goodnight, Dad."

"Good night, Katherine Ann. I'll see you in the morning."

I shuffled back down the hall and climbed into bed. I didn't even realize I had fallen asleep until the sound of shattering glass jolted my heart into my throat as I screamed!

Thirteen

I scrambled out of bed and fell to the floor with a thud. My legs twisted in the blankets. I kicked violently until my feet were free, allowing me to stand. Pain shot up my leg as I put weight on my right foot. I limped toward the bedroom door. Once I was out in the hall, I found my dad's bedroom door closed, which meant my father hadn't heard the glass shattering and was still sleeping.

Holding onto the wall, I made my way to the kitchen. The house was dark, illuminated only by the soft white glow of the moon shining through the kitchen window. I flicked on the kitchen light and scanned the room but found no broken glass. I moved around the counter toward the living room. My father lay on the floor, glass scattered around him.

"Dad," I called, but he didn't answer. He didn't budge. That's why he didn't hear me scream!

I fell to my knees beside him. Blood trickled from a gash on the back of his head. "Dad! Dad, wake up. Oh, my God!"

I shouted, turning him over onto his back. He moaned and slowly opened his eyes.

"Dad, oh thank God, you're okay," I said, my heart racing.

"What... what happened?" he stuttered.

"I don't know. I heard glass shattering and rushed out of my room. That's when I found you here."

"By the time I heard something or someone behind me, I was hit on the head."

"Should I call an ambulance?"

"No, I'm fine. Just help me to the chair."

I wrapped my arm around him and got him into the chair behind us. Then, I scurried to the kitchen, grabbed a dish towel, and ran it under cold water, forgetting all thoughts of my hurt ankle. "Here, put this on your head," I said as I noticed the backdoor ajar.

I helped place the wet towel against the cut on the back of his head, then headed to the open door and peered outside. If someone were out there, they were either hiding in the shadows or long gone. I closed the door, locked it, and walked back to the living room. I began cleaning up the broken glass. "What is all this stuff?" I asked, pointing at the scattered papers on the floor.

"The case I have been working on."

"Do you think someone knew that you had information about this case and broke in here?"

"I'm not sure. Maybe."

Earlier, he hadn't heard me behind him either. What did that mean? I wasn't sure. Maybe he was too immersed in the case and had tuned everything else out. "But how would they know you brought the case home with you? How would they know you have anything here?"

"I don't have the slightest idea. Apparently, they're watching me."

"The backdoor is open. Did you forget to lock it?"

"I guess so. Damn it. I'm really sorry, Katherine… I need to be more careful. God, they could have hurt you or worse." My dad put his head in his hands, allowing the wet towel to fall onto the cushion.

"Dad, I'm fine, really. Besides, Eva was in the room with me. She would have protected me." A wave of heat rushed through my body as if I'd just walked into a sauna. I scanned the room but didn't see the dog anywhere. Usually, she stayed by my side. "Eva, come here, girl."

Nothing.

Standing, I called out again as I raced down the hall to my room. The room was empty. I remembered leaving the door open and ran back to the kitchen, fumbling with the lock. I turned the knob and swung the door open. Eva darted past my legs, nearly knocking me over. Tears welled up behind my eyelids.

"You startled me, girl," I said as I knelt on the floor, placing a hand on each side of her face. I would be lost if anything happened to her. Eva wagged her tail. I kissed her furry forehead, stood up, and moved around the room, gathering all the papers and stacking them in a pile on the coffee table.

"Don't," my dad said.

"Don't what?"

"Don't read them. I can't let you get involved. You can't get tangled up in this mess. Do you hear me? You need to stay out of this, Katherine."

"Sorry, Dad, but I'm already involved. They—whoever they are—came into our house and attacked you. Clearly, someone doesn't want you to uncover the truth about what happened."

I sat back on my heels, debating whether to tell my father everything I knew. Maybe they were after me. I decided against telling him and would keep it to myself. I'd continue doing some investigating of my own. It was clear someone was after me, not my dad.

Fourteen

The following morning, I tossed the covers off to find dirt crumbs rubbed into the fabric of my sheets. I examined my feet and found them mostly clean. How did the dirt get into my bed? I had only gone to the backdoor last night. I glanced down at Eve, who was lying on top of the blankets. Her paws were spotless.

I made my bed with clean sheets, then sat down, contemplating how I would watch Trevor, Paige, Jim, and, of course, Gavin. The four people on my list. The same four names were written on a piece of paper my dad had last night. Coincidence? I don't think so. Now, I was sure they were involved somehow.

But where did that leave Mia? According to Paige and Jim's conversation, Mia had nothing to do with any of it. She hadn't been there that night. It had to be Trevor who asked her to be there at their outing on the bleachers. Though, their morning encounter didn't seem staged to me. Recalling Trevor's reaction when he saw Mia that morning suggested he hadn't seen her in a while, and yet they're back together? I couldn't understand their relationship because it was too confusing for me. Watching my parents together, I realized that people would do almost anything for love, like breaking up with someone to avoid getting hurt in the end. But this wasn't about me or love.

I hadn't shared anything with my dad. It was better that way. The less he knew, the easier it was to lie to him. I hated lying, but it was all for good reasons.

The fact that I had never lied to my father before seemed *too* easy for me. Was he really that gullible? I wasn't sure why I had to lie to him now. Was it because I wanted to solve this case for him or just to solve it for myself? It occupied my mind and distracted me from thinking about Jim and why I felt I couldn't be with him. It also kept me from missing my mom so much. My plan was to find out more about what happened that night, hopefully by the end of the day.

Mia, on the other hand, didn't fit into my plan. She hadn't been at Camp Wilson; she was, I now know, at home contemplating a way to end her life. There had to be more to her story. Something terrible had happened to Mia, but I just wasn't sure what it was yet. I pondered how to find my way back into her life. Was that something I truly wanted to do? We weren't friends for a reason, a reason that Mia made, which ended our long-ago friendship.

I walked into the living room, and my dad was nestled beneath the throw blanket on the sofa. A relaxed smile spread across my face as I observed the rise and fall of his chest. I didn't have the heart to wake him.

Thank God he was fine. I don't know what I would do if I lost him too. Sure, I had relatives to stay with if something happened to him, but this was my dad. I needed him, and he needed me. We were all we had now. I wouldn't let anyone or anything hurt him.

~

I bounded down the two steps of the bus and stood on the sidewalk. It had been three days, yet it felt like déjà vu all over again, just like the first day of school. Students stared at the car in the parking lot—Trevor's car. Instead of Gavin sitting in the passenger seat, it was Mia. They had gotten back together, though I wasn't sure why people were staring at them. This wasn't anything new; they had dated for two and a half years. Everyone knew they would end up together—no doubt they would one day get married. So, what was different this time compared to any other? I didn't know, and I wasn't going to stand out here like the rest of them. No, I had to get to my locker and grab the books for my first-morning class.

Weaving my way through the crowd, I spotted the same kid I had bumped into three days earlier. Actually, he had bumped into me. He stood beside the building, his gaze locked on me. A shiver coursed through my body as if I'd walked through arctic air. I looked away from him and quickened my pace, wanting nothing more than to be inside the school and among my classmates where I'd feel safe.

Once inside the building, lively chatter filled the hall. It was impossible to determine what the conversations were about. Life, I guessed. What do they say, 'never assume'? What could have happened overnight that had my classmates buzzing with excitement?

Well, a lot had happened to me. Like someone breaking into my home and hitting my dad over the head. Someone was watching us—or me; I wasn't sure yet. Was the killer who had murdered that girl now after me? Did that mean one of *them* broke into my house? I clenched my fist as I wondered which of *them* had the audacity to come into my home. I hoped it wasn't Jim.

My mind flicked back to last night. There was no breakage of wood around the door; the frame was intact. So, there were only two possibilities. **One:** my dad had left the door unlocked, though wouldn't he have come in through the garage? **Two:** someone must have used a key to get in, which I was certain had happened unless I forgot to lock the backdoor after letting the dog inside last night. That would then be my fault. Well, there was nothing I could do about it right now. I would look for the key later and remove it from its current hiding spot.

I closed the locker door and turned the corner. Students had formed a roadblock blocking the hallway, and I had no way to get to my class. I quickened my pace and weaved my way to the front of the crowd. Two people stood in the center of the circle: Mia and Trevor. My gaze fell on their fingers, intertwined. I wanted to congratulate myself on getting it right. Those two would always be together.

"Hey, what's going on over here?" Paige asked as she leaned against Jim, who I hadn't realized was standing ten feet to my right. Damn, my pulse raced as blood pumped through my arteries. I needed to stay calm. I swallowed, forcing the lump down. *Calm down.* I closed my eyes, opened them, and exhaled the breath I had been holding.

"I think someone spray-painted Mia's locker," Jim remarked.

"What?!" Paige shrieked. "Who would do something like that? Do you know what it says?"

All Paige had to do was look at the locker instead of my Jim. Then again, I hadn't looked either.

"Slut," Jim muttered.

My head whipped toward the lockers, and sure enough, in black spray paint was the word SLUT. Students began to chatter loudly over one another. I stepped back and took a few strides to the right, now in earshot. I wanted to hear the words exchanged between Jim and Paige as they whispered to each other.

Jim leaned in close to Paige. "My guess would be Gavin."

This didn't surprise me in any way.

"Are you serious right now?" Paige asked.

"I would never lie to you."

Paige smiled and nudged Jim with her arm. "Ah, that's so sweet."

My eyes widened at the words. What did he mean? Were they? Could they be dating, and was Jim lying about it? The thought sickened me. I swallowed the acidic taste rising in the back of my throat, praying Jim wouldn't lean in and kiss Paige right here in front of me. I would lose it if he did. I wouldn't be able to control myself. I would react like a deranged lunatic.

"Okay, what's happening here?" Mr. Nelson asked, making his way through the crowd opposite me. "What the…? Who did this?" Mr. Nelson scanned the faces of those gathered around.

Then another voice shouted, “What on earth! Why would anyone write something so terrible?” Miss Hermon exclaimed as she rushed up beside Mr. Nelson.

“Your guess is as good as mine,” Mr. Nelson said. “Kids these days.”

“Who does this locker belong to?” Miss Hermon asked as her eyes scanned the students hovering around the lockers.

“It’s mine,” Mia whispered.

“Oh, dear Jesus,” Miss Hermon whispered. “Okay. All right. We’ll call the janitor and have this cleaned up for you.”

“Why would anyone call you a *slut*?” Mr. Nelson asked.

Mia stood there, shaking her head back and forth. "I... I don’t know. I didn’t do... I don’t know.” Tears ran down her cheeks.

Her voice cracked as she cried in front of everyone filming her. My gaze went to their hands laced together again. Trevor squeezed her hand, then let go and wrapped an arm around her waist.

“There, there. No one’s accusing you of anything. Come on, I’ll take you to the nurse’s station. You can sit in there until you feel better.” Miss Hermon turned to the students who were standing there. “Okay, let’s go, everyone. Get to class. There’s nothing to see here. We’ll take care of this.” Miss Hermon embraced Mia and guided her away.

Trevor turned and scanned the crowd until he spotted Jim and Paige. He walked over to them, and the three of them proceeded down the hall, away from wandering eyes. This was my chance to find out what was happening. I slithered in behind them. Trevor pulled open the door to the stairwell, and the three of them slipped inside.

I needed to know what they were talking about, but how could I listen this time without getting caught? Then it struck me. I dashed to the janitor's closet beside the stairwell door.

Last year, Jim and I had hidden in this very closet for some alone time. That memory made me smile. The taste of his lips on mine, his hands caressing my back as he held me close. I craved him in that moment, but this wasn't the time to rekindle our love. Besides, he was with *her*. I shook the vision from my mind, glanced over my shoulder, and ducked inside. The school had installed a vent near the ceiling on the wall, allowing you to hear everything said on the other side. I flipped the empty bucket over and climbed on top, stretching my neck to place my ear near the vent.

"What if she says something?" Paige asked. "I'm not going to jail."

"No one's going to jail. She just needs to gather herself. She'll be okay," Trevor replied.

"You'd better hope so," Paige hissed. "I'm not getting into trouble and losing everything I've worked so hard to achieve."

"She better keep her freaking mouth shut!" Jim snapped. "And you all thought I'd say something. Leave it to Mia the spaz to get us all in trouble."

"Stop!" Trevor snapped. "Don't talk about her like that! I'll handle this. No need to get your panties in a twist, you two. I'll head to the nurse's office and speak with Mia."

"Do you think Gavin did this?" Paige asked.

"Well, if he did, he's going to pay. I'm done putting up with that guy!" Trevor growled.

"Wait, aren't you friends with him, Jim?" Paige asked.

"No!" Jim snapped.

"Out of all of us, you know Gavin best. Why don't you find him and tell him to stop? Enough is enough," Paige demanded. "Before someone gets hurt."

"And if he doesn't, we'll make him stop," Trevor added.

"What can I do?" Jim asked.

"Well, you're his ex-best friend; he'll listen to you? Maybe you can blackmail him? Don't you know things about him that could make him stop all of this? "Are there things he doesn't want anyone else to find out?" Paige asked.

"Hey, what are you doing in here?" shouted a voice from the doorway of the janitor's closet.

I whipped my head toward the open door, the light blinding my vision. I jumped down from the bucket, knocking it over. Then, I ran past the janitor, nearly running him over, and sprinted down the hall.

Fifteen

I sped around the corner and leaned against the wall. My heart was racing. With my eyes closed, I took a deep breath. In, out, in, out, until my pulse calmed. The janitor's loud voice echoed in my head like a drill sergeant. I prayed they hadn't heard him, although they wouldn't have known it was me eavesdropping on their conversation. The janitor could have been yelling at anyone from this school. I counted to five in my head, then peeked around the wall. It was empty. "Thank God," I whispered, letting the tension in my neck and shoulders fade away.

I didn't remember hearing the bell ring since the incident occupied my mind. Holding my books against my chest, I pushed away from the wall and walked to class.

I entered the classroom to find that Trevor's seat was empty. Mia had gone to the nurse's office, so where was Trevor? Was he still in the stairwell with the others? I didn't know, but I was sure he'd show up soon unless, of course, he wanted to be with his girlfriend.

"Okay, class. Let's begin by opening our books to page 96," the teacher said. In the first semester, we will study and learn *Differential Calculus*. In the second semester, we will study *Integral Calculus.*"

I half-listened to what he was teaching while my mind kept rewinding to the conversation I had just heard. Could Gavin have really spray-painted that word on Mia's locker? If so, why? What would his reason be? Was everything somehow related to the girl found in the woods, her spirit pulling me toward her? I didn't recall them mentioning anything about her or being at the campsite. It's possible I had it all wrong and they had no connection with the dead girl. My mind could be grasping for something to occupy my time instead of focusing on what was important, like school. Uncertainty spun in my brain. They were up to something; otherwise, why would they be sneaking around?

I replayed, word-for-word, what had been exchanged among the three of them. Yes, Trevor mentioned that he was going to the nurse's office to talk to Mia. But what lingered in my mind was Jim's comment: "Mia better keep her freaking mouth shut!" Mia knew something, and I had to figure out what it was, but that meant I needed to get close to her.

~

Hours ticked away like a wild horse running along the shoreline. There was no sign of Trevor, Paige, Jim, or Mia since this morning—until I walked into the cafeteria. Jim sat alone at a table, eating his bagged lunch that his mom always made. I glanced around the room; the others were nowhere to be seen.

I stepped forward but caught myself. Sitting with Jim would be a bad idea. It would give him the wrong impression, making him think we were getting back together, that we were working things out. Though, if I were completely honest with myself, I wanted to. I missed him—missed spending time with him. He had a way of making me laugh like no one else. But it would be wrong in every sense of the word to drag him along if I couldn't commit my whole heart to the relationship.

Jim stared directly at me. Our eyes locked. My stomach swirled with exhilaration, and my head felt fuzzy. *Stop it, Kat; you can't think about that right now*. I needed to escape. I turned away from his hypnotic gaze and rushed out of the room.

"Kat, wait up!" Jim shouted.

I halted as if I had collided with a brick wall, twisting my neck to peer over my shoulder.

"Hey, can we talk?" Jim asked. "I want to continue our conversation from yesterday."

I didn't. A tingling sensation filled my head from holding my breath. I closed my eyes, released the air from my lungs, and then turned around to face him.

"Oh, uh, now's not a good time, Jim," I replied. My hands instinctively wanted to slip into the back pockets of my jeans, but today, I was wearing leggings, which don't have pockets. I crossed my arms in front of me as my stomach rolled.

"Oh, did you have somewhere to go?"

No. "Yeah, they called me into the office."

"You were? I didn't hear anything over the intercom."

"No, it was last period. My teacher said I needed to go when I had free time," I lied. I guess it has something to do with my college credits." I shrugged my shoulders.

He nodded, accepting my response. "How about after school? Can you talk then?"

Shit! I was totally free. "Actually, my dad has plans for us tonight."

"Are you avoiding me, Kat? If you are, then just say it. I can't let you string me along like a piece of meat left out to dry," Jim said. His bottom lip began to quiver, and his face flushed until it turned beet red.

Technically, I wasn't leading him on because I refused to express my feelings. I uncrossed my arms and turned away from him. My feet were in flight mode; I needed to escape before he realized I was so full of shit he'd never want to talk to me again.

"Sorry, I really have to go. I promise we'll talk soon." The words slipped out before I had time to process what I had just said.

Sixteen

I promise, my mind repeated as I stepped around the corner, away from Jim's watchful gaze. Why in the world did I say that? Eventually, I would have to bare my soul, but I hoped it would be much further in the future.

I regained my composure and stared down the hallway. If I was going to the office, I was going the wrong way, which meant Jim now knew I had lied to him. "Shit," I fumed. Well, I couldn't turn around and head back the other way. Jim, I was sure, stood there waiting for me to realize my mistake. Maybe he was hoping I would so he could corner me again and finally get the truth out of me. The truth was that I still loved him with all my heart but was afraid of losing him forever like I had lost my mom. My mind protested. How stupid it sounded now that I thought about it. But it was my heart I was saving from getting hurt. I didn't. No, I couldn't go through the loss again if one day he decided I wasn't enough for him and walked away.

I ambled down the hall and pushed through a set of double doors. A ray of sunshine warmed my face. I needed a few moments to myself, to breathe without feeling guilty for the pain I had caused Jim and for the pain I had caused myself. He would eventually move on. Oh, wait, he had already— with *her*. With Paige. God, I didn't want to think about it. About them.

Part of me wanted to escape somewhere and forget they existed, but wasn't it me who got them involved? Well, yes, but that was only because I needed an escape. I needed something to help fill the void left by Jim not being in my life. And yet, Jim was involved anyway. Did I think walking away from him would fix everything? Leaving the love of my life and not regretting a single second of what we shared? That he would disappear as if he had never been there? This was too much. If I had known it was going to be this hard, I would have stayed with him. Staying would have been wrong. I would have treated him poorly, and he didn't deserve that. He was too good a guy.

Shouting pricked at my right ear, snapping me back to reality. I followed the noise, the voices growing louder. I trotted down the steps and then along the side of the building. I stopped at the edge of the structure and peered around the corner. Trevor and Jim were having a heated discussion in the teacher's parking lot.

"Look, I told you I would handle it, and I did!" Trevor shouted. "She's not going to say a damn word to anyone."

"I'm glad you think so, but that girl is a ticking time bomb," Jim replied. "Why else would she try to kill herself?"

In that instant, Trevor's arms shot out and pushed Jim to the ground.

"What the hell, man!" Jim shouted back, his nostrils flaring as he sprang to his feet, prepared to fight.

Jim wasn't a fighter, nor did he ever get angry. Whatever was happening with them was certainly changing him into a different person. I needed to stop this before the school principal came outside and handed them both weekend detentions for a month. I stepped out from beside the building but quickly jumped back against the brick wall when another familiar voice rang in my ears.

"Knock it off, both of you. I can't believe you're fighting over this," Paige interrupted. "You're going to get us all into trouble."

Trevor and Jim stared at each other, then Jim waved a hand in the air. "Forget you, man. I don't know why I even bothered wanting to be friends with you." Jim turned and walked away, heading back toward the side entrance of the school.

"I had no idea we were friends," Trevor shouted back.

"You're such an asshole," Paige hissed. "We need him, and all you do is defend your girlfriend. You know she needs help, right?"

"Shut up! You have no idea what you're talking about."

"Don't I?"

"I said shut up!" Trevor stepped closer to her.

"Whatever. What do you care, anyway? Your future is already set in stone," Paige replied, unaware of Trevor's stance.

If Paige doesn't shut up and leave, Trevor will hit her. No matter how much I disliked her, I couldn't just stand by and let that happen.

"Alright! I'll give him some time to cool off, and then I'll take care of it."

"You'd better. We need him to get to Gavin."

"I know, I know. Don't worry about it, Miss Dean's List; I'll have a word with him."

Paige turned around and walked in the same direction Jim had gone, leaving Trevor alone in the parking lot. This was my chance to talk to Trevor—just the two of us. I needed to question him without the others around, to ask him about that night. Was he in those woods, and did he have anything to do with killing that girl? Did Jim or Paige have any involvement? And what about Gavin? What was his role in all of this? Was he there, too?

I stepped away from the building just as Trevor's cell phone rang. He pulled the phone from his front pocket, glanced at the caller ID, and then put the phone to his ear before jogging away.

~

Entering my bedroom, I collapsed onto my bed with a heavy sigh. I had so many missed opportunities today to get the much-needed answers. As usual, I let my emotions get the best of me. Enough, I decided. From this moment on, I will focus only on the case. I would block out everything else until it was solved and the killer was behind bars.

Something bumped against my left leg, and I sat up. Eva sat on the floor, staring at me with those dreamy puppy dog eyes. It was true that no matter how old dogs got, they never lost that look in their eyes, especially when they wanted something. "Hey, pretty girl. You need to go out, don't you?" Eva stood, wagging her tail, and then twirled in a circle.

I stood and walked out of the bedroom to the backdoor. As I reached for the doorknob, my eyes caught something on the floor in front of the door. I knelt down for a closer look. Blood? Was it from last night? I replayed the scene in my mind. My father lay on the floor in the living room. So, how did his blood end up here? I hadn't seen any blood splatter on the walls. Thank God it hadn't been a fatal blow to the head. My mind raced through every scenario. I recalled shattered glass near my father. Did that mean the person who did this cut themselves? "It could be their blood," I whispered.

The dog whined behind me, so I opened the door, and Eva dashed out into the backyard. I hurried down the hall to the bathroom, grabbed a Q-Tip, and rushed back to the kitchen. The blood had dried, and I couldn't swab it with the cotton tip's end. I dashed to the kitchen drawer. Inside, it held various items: papers, pens, scissors, batteries, assorted tools, and razor blades. I picked up the small plastic container of blades and opened it.

I knelt in front of the door and scraped the dry blood into a sandwich bag. *Now what?* my mind wondered. What was I going to do with the sample? Should I give it to my dad and have him run it? But wouldn't he need something to compare it to? He couldn't start swabbing people for their DNA, unless… Unless he could. He had a list of names. He could tell them he needed to rule them out. I would talk to him about it tonight.

The dog barked, and I opened the door, allowing Eva to bound inside. My eyes caught a glimpse of something on the deck. I walked over to investigate. It was the garden sculpture that had belonged to my mother. I bent down and tilted the statue to the side. The extra house key was missing.

Seventeen

I yawned and stretched my arms above my head before sitting up in bed. I glanced at the clock to check the time, but there were no numbers glowing back at me. I threw my legs off the side of the bed and grabbed the clock, pulling the cord along with it. Had I accidentally unplugged it during the night? I shook my head. No, I didn't think so, but I couldn't be certain.

I set the clock back on the nightstand and picked up my cell phone. The phone lit up, displaying the time as a few minutes past two in the morning. I scratched my temple.

From the corner of my eye, a light flickered off from under the door. Was my dad going to sleep now? Last night flashed through my mind, and I quickly stood up, racing toward the door, adrenaline coursing through my body. Something fell to the floor, but I couldn't tell where the noise came from in the house. I waited, pressing my ear against the door, listening for my dad to walk down the hall to his room, which is diagonal from mine, but there was nothing. No floorboards creaked in the hall.

I laced my fingers around the doorknob and turned it. Letting out a breath, I pulled the door toward me just enough for my body to slip through. Then it hit me: I should have grabbed something for protection, just in case it wasn't my father. Well, it was too late now; I had already stepped out into the hall and was facing the kitchen. Like last night, I heard the same *ding* sound. *This time, i*t came from my father's room. If he were in the bedroom, then who was in the kitchen?

I focused on the front of me. Darkness wrapped around me like a blanket. I blinked until shapes formed in front of me. Then, the shuffling of papers crept down the hall and into my ears. It was possible my dad left his cell phone in the bedroom, but why would he be sitting in the dark going through papers? A flash of light followed by darkness. I swallowed, my heart pounding beneath my chest. Someone was in the house again.

I stood in the hall, unsure of what to do, just as Eva pushed past me and dashed toward the kitchen. "No!" I whispered and shouted, but the dog didn't stop. Something crashed to the floor with a *thud,* and then an image flashed across my view into the kitchen. Someone was definitely in the house, and they were running for the backdoor.

I ran down the hall and into the kitchen, flipping on the switch as I entered. Light filled the surrounding space; no one was there, but the backdoor was wide open. The dog came sprinting from the living room and out the door to the backyard. "No," I screamed, but it was too late. The dog was already through the door and outside with the intruder.

"What in the world is happening out here?"

I whipped around to find my dad standing in the doorway of his bedroom. He was wearing a white t-shirt and boxers decorated with pizza slices— a Christmas gift I had given him. I must have woken him, as his hair was disheveled on one side.

"Dad," I gasped. "Someone was in the house again. I heard something and came out to check if it was you. I turned on the light, and Eva ran outside." My body trembled.

"What?" he asked, reaching for something in the room. He emerged with a baseball bat in his left hand and walked past me into the living room.

There was an intruder in our house. Why didn't he grab his gun? Then I remembered that he had locked the gun in a safe near his bed and probably didn't want to waste time retrieving it. Besides, the bat would inflict some damage if the intruder were close enough and didn't have a weapon.

I followed him into the living room, my hand pressed firmly over my mouth to hold back a scream. Someone had ransacked our living room. "Dad?" I asked.

"Damn it!" he muttered.

"Dad, what's wrong?" I stood beside him. "Did they take anything?"

"I don't know." He ran a hand through his hair, then dropped to his knees to gather the papers scattered on the floor.

Scratching filtered into the room. I spun around. Eva stood at the back door, her paw tapping against the wood. The door opened, and she strolled over to me, wagging her tail.

"You can't run after someone like that," I said to the dog, kneeling in front of her. I stroked her head, then stood up and hurried to the door, closed it, and turned the deadbolt. A thought clicked in my mind. "Dad, did you take the key from under the statue?"

"What?" he asked, still picking up papers from the floor.

"The key. I checked earlier under Mom's statue on the back porch, but it's missing. Did you take it?"

"No, I completely forgot we had one hidden out there. Why?"

I needed to tell him now. "It's missing."

"What? Are you sure?"

"Yeah, I looked under everything last night. I couldn't find it anywhere."

"Great!" he muttered quietly. "I suppose I'll need to stop by the hardware store and pick up a new lock for the back door."

"Are you going to report this?"

"I'll take care of it at work tomorrow. I'll inform my Captain that we've been experiencing some break-ins." He rose to his feet, shuffling the handful of papers in his hands. "I'm sorry; I should be more mindful. I shouldn't bring my work home with me."

"Yeah, but who would know about it? How would they know to look in our house? And what could you possibly have that they would want?"

He shrugged his shoulders. "I don't know, honey. I wish I did. If the key is missing, it means they have a way inside. So tomorrow, I'll have the locks changed and maybe add another deadbolt to the back door."

I nodded. "Do you want me to help you?"

"No, I think I have everything. You should go to bed now. I'll handle this."

"Okay, love you."

"Love you too."

I turned and walked down the hall to my room. I wasn't sure, but the only person I ever told about the key being hidden outside lived across the street.

Eighteen

"Hey, Kat, do you have a second?"

I slammed the locker door and turned around. "Christ, you scared me," I shrieked. My hand instinctively flew to my chest.

"I called your name. I guess you didn't hear me."

"Yeah, well, I've got a lot on my mind lately." *Like you breaking into my house last night?*

"Yeah, okay, so I was just thinking if you'd want to come over to my place after school."

My mouth dropped open, but I quickly shut it. Was she serious right now? "I don't understand?"

"Why, is it because we haven't talked in ages?"

I nodded.

"Perhaps it's time to change that."

"Oh."

"You can trust me, Kat. Plus, I believe my parents would be thrilled to see you."

Trust her? I doubt it. It's been over three years, and now she wants to hang out with me. Did Mia really think I was an idiot? I wasn't sure whether to believe her or not. Something was happening, but what better way to keep an eye on the enemy than in her own home?

"Alright, sounds good. After school, at your place."

Mia smiled and said, "Great!"

I slipped past her and walked down the hall. Trevor stood at his locker, staring at Mia. I lifted my head and walked by him. The more I considered the idea, the more it dawned on me that Mia wasn't the one in my home last night or any other night. Maybe she took the key, but I have no doubt she gave it to Trevor. Was this a scheme to keep me out of my house while he searched it? My dad would have all the case files with him, so what was the point of searching my home? I didn't know this, but I had an idea.

~

"Covinski, it's so nice of you to join us!" Mr. Miller said. "I didn't think Sociology was your cup of tea?"

My head snapped up from the textbook. Why was Jim switching to Sociology?

"So, tell me, Covinski, what makes you want to take my class?"

Jim's face flushed red as he stood at the front of the class. He cleared his throat. "To learn more about relationships."

Everyone in the class laughed except me. I stared at him, astonished that he would volunteer for this class.

"Well, you will definitely learn about them in what we call life. Please take a seat next to Miss Palmer."

I swallowed. *Yeah, why not have my ex-boyfriend sitting right next to me? Good thinking, Mr. Miller.*

Jim sauntered down the aisle and took the empty chair next to mine. He flashed me a smile and placed his backpack on the floor beside the chair. He kept his eyes on me the entire time until a heavy thud made him jump in his seat. Jim jerked his head up to see Mr. Miller dropping a textbook onto his desk.

"There won't be any problems sitting next to Miss Palmer, right?"

"No, sir."

"Great! Let's start by turning to page 34 in our books. This week, we'll be reading about social interactions."

I stared at the pages of my book. What was he doing here? He really didn't want to learn about sociology, did he? Well, I wasn't going to ask him; that would just give him another reason to talk to me.

Almost an hour later, the bell rang, and I collected my belongings.

"Hey, do you want to be study buddies?" Jim asked.

I turned to him and stared. "You're joking, right? Mr. Miller hasn't even assigned us anything yet, and you want to study together?"

"Kat, I always want to be with you, whether we're studying or not."

My heart filled with warmth. It was the sweetest thing anyone had ever said to me, but this wasn't the right time. He was a suspect in a girl's murder. Didn't he know that? My eyes fell to the floor, then back up to him. "Jim, were you at Camp Wilson over the summer? A few weeks ago?"

He nodded.

"Were you there when that girl was killed?"

His brow furrowed.

"Do you know about the girl who was killed in those woods?"

He didn't say anything.

Why wasn't he speaking? "Did you kill that girl?"

"What? No, I didn't kill any girl. I had nothing to do with whatever you're talking about, Kat! How can you even think that I did?" His voice rose with each word. His eyes scanned the room and then returned to me. "You know, for someone who doesn't want to be with me, you sure are curious about what I've been up to lately." He slowly shook his head in disbelief and marched out of the classroom.

My stomach sank as I stood there. Seconds later, I grabbed my books and walked out of class. Why did I think he could kill someone? Now that I had asked him about it and seen his reaction, he would never, ever talk to me again. I was certain of that. *Great job, Kat! What a way to screw things up with the man you love. Accusing him of murder means you'll be alone forever.* Truth be told, hearing him say he had nothing to do with it made me feel more at ease. But the question still remained: if he didn't, then who did?

Nineteen

"I need to let the dog out first; then I'll come over," I said, standing next to Mia on the sidewalk in front of her house.

"Sure, I'll keep the door unlocked. Come in when you're done."

I crossed the street and hurried up the porch stairs. Once inside the house, I dashed to my room and grabbed my video camera. It had belonged to my mom, and my dad had given it to her as a gift. She wanted to capture every moment of my growth.

As I headed back into the living room, I hid the camera on the bookshelf and directed it at the back door. Once I was done taking Eva out, I would hit record and leave through the front door to Mia's. Tonight, I hoped to discover who was in my house, but that was only if they returned again.

I turned the knob to the front door of Mia's house and stepped inside. After closing the door behind me, I stood facing the hall. The same hall I had walked down many times on my way to the stairs that led to Mia's bedroom. Mia, who used to be my best friend, was someone I could count on and talk to about anything. Where did it all go wrong between us? I didn't know why it happened. In all honesty, I never confronted Mia about what she did to me back then. If I had, would we still have remained friends? I honestly don't know.

I drew a breath and then exhaled, allowing my shoulders to fall back and the day's tension to fade. I slinked down the hall and stopped outside the living room. I surveyed the room. Nothing had changed. They hadn't updated their furniture or moved any of their belongings. To me, it remained the same home I had come to love over all the years Mia and I were friends. We had been friends since we were five, attending kindergarten at Hoffman Young Elementary School. We practically did everything together until that one day that destroyed our friendship forever.

My eyes wandered around the open living room, and a memory flashed back to me. Mr. and Mrs. B, which was what I used to call them instead of their full last name, Barnes, were sitting on the beige sofa. They were laughing, and Mr. B pulled his wife closer, hugging her tightly. The love they shared was something I, at fourteen, always hoped I would find one day. My heart ached, and I rubbed my hand over my chest before turning away.

I took a step. The floorboard creaked as my weight shifted, and I stopped. No, it wasn't the floorboard under my foot, but the one above me. Mia's bedroom was directly above. My eyes darted in every direction, but no one was there. It was just me. Why did Mia invite me here? Was it to keep me out of my house while someone rummaged through it? Maybe I should just leave and go back home to catch them in the act?

"Hey, you made it," Mia called from the top floor landing. "I thought you might have changed your mind and decided not to come."

I jumped slightly, letting out a soft chuckle. "No, of course not," I lied, adding a smile to reassure her.

"Good." A smile brightened her face.

The late afternoon sun shone through the octagon window above her head. The light gleamed all around her like an angel. She looked stunning, but Mia usually did. Did she really need me? Want me here with her? Maybe she had changed, and we could be friends again. Did I want to be friends with her again? That was the real question, wasn't it? What Mia had done was unforgivable, wasn't it? Though it was a long time ago; well, not that long ago. No one had even asked me why we weren't hanging out anymore. Did they really care at all?

"Look," Mia said, now standing on the second-to-last step at the bottom of the stairs. "I know I should've said this to you years ago, but..." She shrugged her shoulders. "So much has happened in the last three years, and I should have apologized to you for what happened."

I pushed down the anger and hurt from that day, keeping it where it belonged. I couldn't let it fester and ruin this moment. I had waited three years for this day—waiting for the most popular girl at Hoffman High to stand in front of me and say she was sorry.

"Look, I'm sorry. I know you cared about him a lot, but you need to understand that I didn't plan it. I was waiting for you when he approached me. He mentioned that he had been waiting for a chance to be alone with me, and suddenly, he kissed me. He kissed me, Kat," Mia emphasized. "After I pushed him away, I saw you running the other way through the gymnasium doors. I called out to you, but I don't think you heard me."

"I heard you," I whispered as the pieces of that terrible day rushed back to the forefront of my mind.

"Besides, Jacob is a douche. He wouldn't have been good for you. He was only..."

"He was just out to get into as many girls' pants as he could," I interrupted.

"Yes, exactly. And I want you to know that nothing ever happened between us. I never slept with him. You have to believe me."

"Do I?"

"Of course! You're my best friend."

"*Was* your best friend."

Mia frowned. "Okay, I was, but… that's why I asked you to come here. I want to start over."

"Start over?" I asked.

"Yeah," Mia nodded. "I'm with Trevor, and I love him. There's nothing I wouldn't do to earn your forgiveness for what that jerk did to you—to us. To our friendship."

I laughed. "He's a jerk, huh?" Mia chuckled along with me, and it felt like no time had passed between us. Like two strangers passing in the night. It wouldn't be exactly the same, but Mia did wholeheartedly love Trevor. I wouldn't do anything to jeopardize their relationship. "Okay, but this doesn't mean I fully trust you again. It…"

"I know it will take some time," Mia said with a giggle. "We'll get through it together."

I stood there for a few seconds, soaking in her words. Could this be real? I hoped so. Unlike Jim, I had to take a leap of faith because, to be honest, I missed my best friend.

Twenty

"Hey," Mia began. "Why don't you stay for dinner tonight? I'm sure my parents would love to have you."

"Sure, that sounds good," I replied. My gaze shifted from the book in my lap to the raised scars on her wrists. My throat tightened as I swallowed. I let my mind flash back to the school restroom a few days earlier. Mia stood at the sink, and I remembered how skinny she looked. Initially, I assumed she had become anorexic or bulimic. Then I read that note about what she had done. Now, after seeing the scars on her wrists, I realized it was something serious. I had never in my life believed she would try to take her own life. What had she been thinking and feeling at that moment? What had driven her to want to die?

I couldn't just ask her directly, could I? If we had still been friends, would Mia have confided in me? Would she have shared that she wanted to end her life? My mind spun with confusion. Trevor was the love of her life, so why would she want to end it? What happened that was so awful, so tragic, that living felt impossible?

"Kat, hello. Are you still there?" Mia asked, waving her hand in front of my face.

I raised my head. "What?"

"You were, like, out there somewhere. I called your name, but you seemed lost." Mia looked down at her lap. She tugged the fabric of her shirt sleeve down, slipping her thumb into an opening at the end of her long sleeves. "Oh, uh."

I extended my hand and placed it on her arm. "You don't have to tell me unless you want to."

Mia sat staring at the comforter on the bed. "I… I can't. I'm not ready to tell anyone."

"Did Trevor hurt you in some way?"

Mia shook her head. "No, Trevor would never hurt me."

"Does Trevor know what happened?"

Once more, she shook her head.

"Did someone else do something to you?" The words burst from my lips.

"I'm sorry, I can't," she said as she jumped off the bed.

"I'm sorry. I shouldn't have asked." My head spun as she rushed into the bathroom, shutting the door behind her.

I fell back against the bed and stared at the ceiling. *Why did I say that? Why couldn't I keep my mouth shut for once?*

I would give Mia some time; besides, we had just started talking again today. That didn't mean we were best friends again. It didn't rewind time to when we used to sit and talk about everything and anything. Maybe one day soon she'd tell me what happened to her and why she did what she did, hoping she wouldn't try it again.

I wouldn't say another word about the scars. I'd wait for Mia to come to me. Did I really think we would just slip back into our old relationship as if nothing had happened? Years had passed, and I was sure that Mia believed she had a good reason for ending her life— a reason I didn't know but wanted desperately to uncover. The note I had found included a line that haunted me: *I know I can count on you to keep my secret. Our secret.* Our secret? If the note wasn't from Trevor, then who? That's what I needed to discover, but how? Where would I even begin?

~

"This tastes wonderful, Mrs. B," I said from across the table. Mrs. B nodded but avoided eye contact with me. Maybe it had been a mistake for me to stay? Perhaps Mrs. B didn't want me in her house, eating her food. Did she hold me responsible for what happened to Mia? No, of course not. We hadn't been friends. Maybe she didn't realize we weren't friends anymore, just like my dad didn't know.

"Yes, this is one of her best dishes. We don't have it often," Mr. B said, clearing his throat before taking a sip from his glass.

The atmosphere in the room felt congested and dry. No one was talking but me, which made me uncomfortable. What could I talk about that would distract them from what their daughter had done? Are they ignoring what happened? I didn't know, but they were doing a good job of not communicating.

"How is Dave doing these days? We don't see him very often," Mr. B asked.

I swallowed the sweet, iced tea I had taken a sip of and set my glass back down on the table. "Oh, he's good. Busy as always."

"Is he currently working on a new case?"

My brows knitted together. Why would he ask something like that? I gathered my thoughts before glancing at Mr. B. "Yeah, I think it was the one about the girl who was killed near Camp Wilson."

Mrs. B's fork slipped from her hand and clanged against the side of her plate. "I'm sorry," she murmured, quickly grabbing the fork before it fell to the floor. Her fingers wrapped around the stem of her wineglass pressed it to her lips and drained the contents. It was her second glass of wine in less than fifteen minutes.

I could hardly hear her words as she finished her drink. I looked up and smiled, taking a bite of my food.

“Oh, well, I guess he’s really busy then,” Mr. B said, jumping back into the conversation. "Do you have any idea who might have done it?”

“Dad!” Mia shouted.

Ignoring his question, I chewed and swallowed. “How’s Ethan doing? I haven't seen him.” I thought he’d be home from college for the summer.” *Except summer was over, stupid.*

This time, Mrs. B’s fork slipped from her hand and bounced off the plate onto the floor. She stood up and dashed out of the room. Her heels clicked on the wooden steps as she raced up the stairs. The door slammed shut, leaving just the three of us sitting awkwardly around the table.

Great way to waltz back into their lives, Kat. “Did I say something wrong?” I glanced from Mia to Mr. B, who had his head down and focused on his dinner. “Is everything alright?” I asked. Ethan was Mia’s older brother. The last time I saw him, he had left for Ohio State, but that didn’t seem right. I was sure I had seen his car parked at the curb down the road the other day. But I guess I could have been mistaken.

The room remained silent.

“Mr. B, is everything all right?”

"What?" he asked, his voice rising. "Why would you ask that question?"

I swallowed the lump in my throat. "I'm sorry. I didn't mean anything by it," I whispered, eager to understand why Mrs. B was acting this way. What the hell was going on in this house? Tension filled the room, the air around me thick and suffocating. Did it have anything to do with Mia? Or the girl in the woods? Or her brother, Ethan? Mrs. B stormed out of the room the moment I mentioned Ethan. Or maybe it was because the girl in the woods had died. Was killed. I didn't know, and Mr. B wasn't going to tell me anything.

"Kat, I think it's time for you to go. Mia needs to get ready for school tomorrow and…" He stopped talking as if lost for words.

My stomach twisted into a sailor's knot, one that I feared wouldn't untie. Reluctantly, I pushed my chair back and stood up from the table. "Sure, okay." I lifted my plate off the table.

"Just leave the plate. We'll take care of the table."

I smiled at Mia. "I guess I'll see you at school tomorrow."

"Yeah, tomorrow," Mia frowned.

I was certain she didn't want me to leave, but Mr. B made it perfectly clear that I had to go. After pushing my chair in, I walked down the hall. Once I reached the front door, I glanced over my shoulder but couldn't see either of them. No sounds came from the dining room. Were they waiting for me to leave? Well, their wish was granted. I opened the door and stepped out into the night.

Twenty-One

I lay awake as the sun peeked through the slats of the horizontal blinds covering my bedroom window. I didn't sleep well; in fact, I tossed and turned all night, my mind replaying the few hours I spent next door, a house I never imagined I'd step foot in again.

Mrs. B had been acting strangely as if her world had been turned upside down. In every way, Mrs. B's life had shifted and come crashing down. Her daughter had attempted to take her own life, and as a mother, she was devastated. I would feel the same if it were my daughter, even though I didn't know the full story of what had happened in their house.

Thinking of my own mother and how shattered my heart was when she passed away. Yes, I could relate to what Mrs. B was feeling. But Mrs. B was the lucky one. Mia was still here and not gone like my mom. So, why was she so jumpy? The moment I mentioned the dead girl, she dropped her fork, and then again when I brought up Ethan.

I wasn't sure how the dead girl fit into their lives. Did they know her? Maybe it was because of what Mia did that startled her. Nah, I wasn't buying that. There was something happening in that house. Something connected to Mia's suicide attempt. I was certain of it; I needed to find out what it was.

There was a reason Mia did what she did. You don't just wake up one morning and say, "I think I'm going to kill myself today." You must have had thoughts of suicide, right? It doesn't happen overnight. The truth was, I didn't know. I had never contemplated taking my own life. It must have been bad if Mia couldn't talk about it. I suppose that doesn't mean much. Maybe she didn't want to relive the details of that awful night. To be honest, we hadn't hung out in years. So, if Mia was sad over the summer or something had happened between her and Trevor, though she claimed it had nothing to do with him, I wouldn't have known, would I? No, because we weren't friends, and I wasn't there.

I believed it had nothing to do with Trevor. They were so in love, and Mia was always smiling and laughing. She was full of life, so the question still remained: *"What had happened?"* Had there been someone else? I shook my head; no, that I was sure wasn't the case. Mia wouldn't do that to Trevor, but the truth was, I didn't know the new Mia. Anything could have happened. To be honest, we were both different people now.

I bolted up in bed as if awakening from a nightmare. I

had completely forgotten about the video recorder. I tossed the blankets aside, slipped my feet into my slippers, and hurried out of my bedroom and down the hall to the living room.

"Shit," I cursed. The camera wasn't on the shelf. I searched everywhere on the bookcase. It was gone. Where had the camera gone? I was sure I had placed it right there on the fifth shelf, facing the back door. It couldn't have been a figment of my imagination.

I walked a few steps to the sofa and sank into the fluffy, soft cushions. Staring up at the ceiling, my mind whirled like an old movie projector. I took a moment to organize my thoughts. Was I missing something? The camera wasn't where I had left it, which meant someone must have taken it, but who? Did someone break into our home again while I was next door? Maybe they had noticed the red light and took the camera to eliminate the evidence.

"Katherine, what are you doing?" my father asked.

His voice made my heart skip a beat. I really needed to stop panicking. Lately, I had been jumping at every movement, which was so unlike me. I turned my head toward the kitchen. "Hey, Dad. I was just sitting here thinking." I smoothed a hand over my pajama pants as if to remove a wrinkle that wasn't there.

"Okay?" he questioned.

"It's nothing. I'm just having a hectic week at school." *That's an understatement.*

He nodded and walked over to the coffeemaker. He set a K-Cup in the dispenser.

"Could you make me one of those, too, please?" I asked.

"That kind of morning?"

You have no idea. I stood and walked to the kitchen counter. Eva staggered down the hall, looking haggard. "Good morning, pretty girl," I said to the dog. Eva leaned against my leg. I petted her head and then headed to the back door to let her outside. I unbolted both deadbolts and turned the knob. I shivered and rubbed my arms for warmth as the cool morning air bit at my skin. My eyes fell on the mat on the deck. My camera. How did it get there? I twisted and peered over my shoulder. My dad wasn't paying attention to me or what was outside. I reached down and grabbed the camera just before Eva burst through the door, past me, and down the stairs.

I stood and scanned the backyard. Two years ago, we fenced in our yard, so if someone were hiding outside, I would see them. There would be nowhere for them to hide. Besides, Eva would have sensed them—I was sure of it—or maybe she had, and that was why she flew past me.

I slipped the camera under my T-shirt just as the dog came barreling up the stairs and into the house. "I'll be right back," I said as I shut the door and rushed down the hall to my bedroom.

Once I was inside, I shut the door and pulled the camera from under my shirt. As I fumbled, I hit the eject button, and the side panel opened. "Son of a monkey's ass," I swore. They took the tape.

My body sank into the mattress as I sat on the edge of my bed, staring at the video camera. I had no evidence of who was behind this. They were clever; I'll give them that. They must have known to look for a camera, or they had seen the red light. Why hadn't I turned on the living room light? Or even the kitchen light? Well, it was because I had been in a hurry and wanted to get over to Mia's house.

Then it hit me. This could be a good thing. If this person knew I was onto them, it meant they were watching me, too. Out of the five people, it wasn't Mia, which left Trevor, Jim, Paige, and Gavin. One of them was responsible for this, and I had to find out who.

Twenty-Two

It wasn't easy, but I watched all five of them, mostly as we passed each other in the hall. Whenever I was near one of them, they looked in the opposite direction. Something was brewing. They were planning something, and I had to be ready. None of the other students noticed that anything was off. Apparently, they didn't see the same breadcrumbs I did.

Trevor remained silent during Calculus class. Not that he had ever talked or participated in class, to begin with. The entire time, he glanced over at Mia, who now sat next to him. Once class was over, Mia and Trevor grabbed hands and practically raced out of the room. I followed them down the hall until they disappeared from sight. I then had to circle back to get to my next class.

Paige texted nonstop during English Literature. Was Trevor on the other end? She turned it away from my view so I couldn't read the messages from my seat. It was like she knew I had read her text the other day. Well, she better hope it wasn't Jim on the other end of that phone. I wanted to tell her to stay the hell away from him, but he wasn't mine to claim.

I lost track of Paige between classes until I spotted her later chatting with Mia near the library. They were keeping an eye on me, so I couldn't get close enough to hear what they were discussing. It seemed to be my knack for the day—never close enough to hear, only to watch. I didn't want to look conspicuous and pretended to read the bulletin board where I was standing.

Mia ignored me all day. I guess we weren't friends after all. Maybe she was using me. Blood pulsed in my ears like a raging river. Why doesn't she want anyone to know we're friends again? Am I beneath her standards? Not popular enough for her to hang out with at school? Or maybe she wants me to herself—a secret friend.

The camera flashed in my mind. Looking back, I believe she only invited me over to keep me out of the house while someone searched my home and found the camera. Of course, I hadn't seen the camera outside last night because I took the dog for a walk out the front door and completely forgot about it until this morning. My mind had been elsewhere. I overlooked it because it wasn't there for me to notice when I walked past the bookcase. People tend to forget things all the time if the object isn't visible.

As for her mom, something wasn't right with Mrs. B.

There was more hidden behind those walls in that house than we all knew. A secret lay trapped behind closed doors, alongside its painted walls and delicately arranged possessions. A secret that needed to be released. Perhaps not for everyone to know, but for someone to hear the pain it held and set it free. If Mia talked to me, I would surely ask her why her mother had acted the way she did.

I looked up at Mia, who flashed me an Oscar-winning smile before turning and walking away, leaving me behind yet again. Why had I let her pull me back in once more? I'm so foolish when it comes to her.

As for Jim, he kept glancing over his shoulder whenever he was at his locker or walking down the hall. I hid around the corner and observed him at his locker. Did he sense my watchfulness? His body stiffened, and he whipped his head around, looking for someone. What reason did he have to be scared? Jim was terrible at keeping secrets. I bet he was ready to burst like a balloon.

He shuffled through the books in his locker, closed the door, and headed in the opposite direction. I weaved between the other students lingering in the hallway, keeping several paces behind Jim. He paused and glanced over his shoulder. I ducked behind a tall guy from the basketball team. Once Jim slipped through the door to his next class, I sprinted past and headed down the hallway to mine.

After lunch, there were three classes remaining, one of which was with Jim. Maybe I could persuade him to talk to me. However, after our last conversation, I doubted he would. Still, I would try anyway. What did I have to lose? I needed to get close enough to find out if they were planning something.

As for Gavin, he followed Trevor around like a lovesick puppy. Didn't he realize Trevor wanted nothing to do with him? He couldn't be that clueless, could he? Well, this was Gavin we were talking about. Trevor didn't even acknowledge him, completely ignoring Gavin.

The first day of school came back to me. Why had Gavin been in Trevor's car? I never found out. It couldn't be that Trevor gave him a ride, could it? Sure, but I don't think so. They didn't even live close to each other. There had to be more to it. Trevor was a jock who picked on Gavin, so why would he suddenly be nice to him? The only reason I could think of was that Gavin had something on Trevor and was blackmailing him. So, maybe I should follow Gavin around. I was certain I could get him to talk. He might act all high and mighty around Trevor, but he would crumble if I got him alone.

Twenty-Three

When the two-thirty bell rang, I collected my belongings, rushed to my locker, and hurried to the main entrance at Trevor's locker. It's the same place where Mia met him every day after school.

As I was about to turn down the hall, I stopped and stepped back, hiding around the corner. I pressed my back against the wall, my heart thumping faster and faster. Had he seen me? I didn't think so. I twisted my neck and peeked around the painted brick wall. Fifteen feet away stood Trevor and Gavin. Trevor's fist was clenched at his side as if he were about to punch Gavin in the face. My eyes dropped to the floor, where I spotted a red Slurpee splattered all over the ground at Gavin's feet. His new white suede shoes were now covered with red splotches. My ears perked up, and I looked back at Trevor and Gavin.

"Never show your face around me again," Trevor growled, slamming Gavin's head into the locker.

The *bang* ricocheted through the hall. I flinched and scanned the hallway, examining the faces of the other students, but no one seemed to care about what was happening, as if it were just another normal day at Hoffman High. Trevor grabbed Gavin's T-shirt, pulling him in close. They were now just inches apart, their noses nearly touching. Were they about to kiss like lovers after a quarrel?

"Don't say a damn word, you hear me? Stay the hell away from me and Mia, or I'll end you," Trevor snarled. Spit flew from his mouth, spraying in all directions. He shoved Gavin against the locker and stormed away.

I gasped at Trevor's words. *He wouldn't, would he?* But I couldn't worry about Trevor right now. I had to follow Gavin. I needed to find out what was going on between the two of them. Why was Trevor so angry with him? What did Gavin know that Trevor didn't want others to know? My mind scanned through every scenario I'd seen and heard this week. There had been a lot of things, and I couldn't be sure if there were any new rumors circulating around the school.

I peered around the corner. Gavin smoothed his now-wrinkled shirt. He lifted his head to scan the hall, but no one was paying him any attention.

Only me.

No one cared what happened to Gavin, though I can't blame them because he brought situations upon himself. No one acknowledged that there was even a confrontation in the hall. *Typical.* Not like Mia's locker, which was spray-painted with the word SLUT on it. That happened first thing in the morning. It was after two-thirty in the afternoon, and most of the students were outside, getting on the bus to go home. This school was so poorly run that the faculty couldn't see what went on here. They want to ignore the abuse and violence, covering up everything that happens as if it were a "Leave It to Beaver" episode.

I shook my head and looked back at Gavin. He stared down at his feet and stepped away from the spilled mess on the floor. He didn't even clean it up; instead, he walked toward the exit doors leading to the parking lot. This was my chance to follow him. I pushed off the wall and bolted around the corner, colliding into someone. I stepped back. "Sorry. I'm so sorry. I didn't mean to…" My voice trailed off as my eyes adjusted. "Mia?"

"What are you doing?" she asked.

My head tilted slightly to the right. "What? What do you mean? I'm leaving school," I said in a frazzled tone.

"I saw you peeking around the corner, watching Gavin."

"And that's a crime?" I asked, hugging my books tightly to my chest. "It's not like your boyfriend was being discreet. Anyone could have heard what he said to Gavin. Then what?"

"What did he say?"

Should I tell her? Knowing something she didn't gave

me an advantage, but I was certain she would ask Trevor, and he would tell her anyway. "That he will end him if he talks. What exactly does he know?"

She glanced down at the floor, then back up again. Her eyes shifted side-to-side as if she were concocting a lie. "What are you implying? Trevor would never intentionally hurt anyone."

"What? Do you want me to spell it out for you, Mia?"

"Oh, stop it, Kat! I'm not going to argue with you here. I thought we could be friends again, but you keep snooping into things that aren't your business." She poked me in the chest with her index finger.

"Excuse me?" I took a step back from her.

"You heard me! Stop sticking your nose where it doesn't belong."

"Why don't you tell me what's going on, and then I won't have to."

Mia let out a heavy sigh, allowing her shoulders to slump. She glanced around and then turned back toward me. "Look," she whispered. "Please, just let it go. I don't want you getting tangled up in this mess. Believe it or not, Kat, I care about you. This thing." Mia swirled a finger in the air. "Doesn't involve you, so do yourself a favor and let it go. I'm begging you."

I stared at her, waiting for more, but instead, she turned

around and walked away, heading down another hallway rather than out the doors to the parking lot where the students parked. I didn't waste another second standing there like an obedient dog; I followed her.

I spotted her up ahead and moved faster, weaving through the crowd of students still gathered in the halls. I stopped in my tracks. Paige closed the locker door and turned around; her posture stiffened before crumbling beneath her blouse.

"Come with me," Mia insisted.

Paige grumbled something I couldn't catch. She didn't want to go with Mia, but she followed her anyway down the hall and out a different door. Where were they headed? I broke into a jog toward the exit.

"No running, Miss Palmer!" Mr. Miller shouted from the open doorway.

Ignoring him, I hurried down the hall, pressed hard on the door release, and stepped outside. Brightness pierced my eyes. I blinked several times until the spots faded away. I glanced to the left and then around the door to the right. Paige had vanished around the corner. I raced to the edge of the building and peeked around the corner. They were walking toward Trevor's car. Of course, who else would they be here to meet?

"Get in," Mia commanded, opening the passenger door

and folding the seat forward.

I had so many questions but didn't know how to find the answers. They were leaving, and I had no way to follow them. I didn't have a car.

Paige ducked and squeezed between the seats. Her head appeared in the rear window, but someone else was in the backseat with her. The person turned and stared at Paige. My stomach dropped. Jim was in the backseat with her.

Mia turned and spotted me, then pushed the front seat back and climbed inside. Trevor started the car and backed out of the spot. He drove away from the school, heading in the opposite direction from where they all lived. He was driving out of town, away from prying eyes. My prying eyes. I didn't have the slightest idea where they were going. What was I going to do now? I had no way to follow them. "God, why won't my dad get me a damn car?" I muttered to myself.

I left the side of the building and started down the sidewalk. Since I missed the bus, I had to walk home. I spent the entire time piecing everything together, which I had been doing since I saw the newspaper with the dead girl's picture on the front cover. What was I missing? Who was that girl? And why was she killed? I, of course, didn't have those answers. But I knew who did, and they had just left.

In Trevor's car.

I was certain they knew the truth about what happened

to her, to the dead girl.

I stopped on the sidewalk in front of my house. The hair on my arms stood on end as if I had walked through a magnetic field. My stomach churned. I turned and scanned the surroundings, but I didn't see anyone. I couldn't see Gavin's car. Maybe he wasn't in it; perhaps he was on foot. Yet, I hadn't seen a single person out here with me. A squeal pierced my ear. I whipped around to see a woman jogging down the sidewalk, pushing a stroller. The baby squawked again.

The fear drained from my body. I twisted around and strolled up the path to my front door. Half an hour later—though I definitely wasn't watching the clock and counting the minutes—a car door slammed shut. I raced to my bedroom window and peered outside. Mia stood on the sidewalk as Trevor drove away. She turned toward my house, looking right at me. I ducked behind the curtain, but I was sure she had spotted me.

Twenty-Four

Later that night, as I lay beneath the blankets staring at the ceiling, headlights appeared. Normally, I wouldn't have cared, but these lights flashed off, then on, and then off again, like a signal.

I sprang out of bed and hurried to the window. Kneeling, I peered out into the night. My eyes darted quickly, scanning every shadow and flicker of movement. I didn't spot the car right away. The dark shadows of the trees concealed the car from view. His car sat in the exact same spot where I had presumably seen Ethan's car a few days ago.

The interior light flicked on inside the car, revealing his location. Squinting, I peered through the darkness toward Mia's house and saw her climbing out of the bedroom window. She darted across the roof and down the trellis on the side of the house, just like she did when she snuck out and came into my room when we were younger.

Once on the ground, she jogged across the yard toward the parked car. I was fairly certain it was Trevor's car, but I couldn't be sure. I couldn't see who was inside or the model of the car, but who else could it be?

Not wasting any more time, I quickly put on jeans and a shirt and slipped my feet into sneakers. I opened the window, grateful that it didn't squeak, and threw my legs over the windowsill, jumping down to the ground below.

I closed the window and stepped to the left, hiding behind the massive bush my dad had planted along the perimeter of our house. Using my fingers, I pushed down on the twisted branches. The car moved forward with its headlights off. Once under the streetlight, Trevor's red Honda Prelude came into view, revealing two other silhouettes in the back seat. Jim and Paige? Yes, I was sure it was them.

Before leaving my bedroom, I grabbed my set of car keys. I ran to the car and threw open the door, placing the key in the ignition. I turned the key once, pressed on the brake, released the parking brake, and put the car in neutral. The car coasted down the incline and onto the street. I had never done this before, but it worked like a charm in movies.

Once on the road, I started the car and drove off, hoping that it wasn't too late, and they weren't too far ahead of me. I spotted the taillights and slowed down, staying back a far distance so they wouldn't spot me. Although they didn't know I was following them. At least, I wished that wasn't the case. I was driving with no headlights on.

They drove for a while, and then Trevor's car turned right. I kept on driving. I didn't want to look suspicious if I, too, turned down the same road. Besides, I'd have to flip on my headlights to see where I was going.

Caution tape lay slack across the gravel road leading to the campsite. The cabins came into view, and I parked the car, turning off the engine. The headlights flickered off, plunging me into total darkness. Climbing out of the car, I scanned the buildings.

The ones at Camp Wilson.

Something had happened here, but what? According to the newspaper, the police hadn't found out who did it. Who killed that poor, innocent girl? Though, to be honest, I had no idea if she was truly innocent. Still, the girl didn't deserve to die, did she?

I used the flashlight on my phone and walked toward the trees on the other side of the cabin. There were several picnic tables and a man-made firepit to my right. Mosquitoes whined in my ear, and I swatted them away. The path was up ahead, but it would take me over fifteen minutes to reach the spot where the girl was killed or at least where she was found dead. I wasn't sure if she had died there. What if the killer brought her to that spot? I was letting my mind wander again, something I did too often these past few days.

A chill ran down my spine, causing me to shiver. There

wasn't much of a breeze in these woods—no branches moving or leaves fluttering in the wind. So, why was I suddenly feeling cold?

The hairs on my arms stood on end as a ghostly feeling washed over me like I had been here before. In this exact spot. My body jolted. I wasn't sure where I was, but it was dark like a raven's wing. It was so dark I couldn't see my hand in front of my face. Whispers filled my ears, murmuring words to me. I spun around but saw no one. There was no one out here with me. My head jerked as if I had nodded off. I rubbed my hands up and down my arms to warm myself. *What just happened to me?*

What was I thinking, being out here alone in these woods? Well, not completely alone; they were here somewhere. The four of them. Doing what, I don't know. Maybe I had gotten it wrong? Maybe they went to a different spot? They had turned onto the road that led into Lemmon's Park, which was less than a quarter of a mile away from where I was. I stood listening to the sounds around me. Where were they? Then, in the distance, I heard car doors slamming shut.

I moved toward the sound. In these woods, it was too difficult to be quiet. Branches and dried pine needles snapped and crunched under my feet. I wanted to use the light from my cell phone but didn't want to give myself away. They couldn't know I was here, that I had followed them. Besides, I didn't want to find out what they'd do to me if they discovered I was out here spying on them.

With a cautious step, I moved toward their voices. I needed to be careful. In these woods, treacherous hills and cliffs surrounded me. I couldn't see where I was going, and I could end up dead, with no one knowing I was out here.

I shook my head, not wanting to think about what had happened out here weeks ago, but the dead girl returned to my mind once more. Had she been out here for a while? My thoughts drifted back to the article; I wasn't sure. My dad had filled me in on what they found at the scene.

I stopped in my tracks, tilting my head toward the voices. I was getting closer—so close that the hairs on my arms stood up, almost saluting. After a few more hesitant steps, their silhouettes came into view. A massive stump about four feet high and two feet wide stood before me. I crouched down behind it. Bats flapped their wings overhead, flying from tree to tree. I closed my eyes, cringing at the sound of them zipping through the air, hoping they wouldn't fly at me.

Trevor spoke first: "We're going to be hiding over here. We will be able to hear every word he says."

"Alright," another voice responded.

I was certain it was Jim. But who were they talking about? Gavin? Were they here to trap him? To make him keep quiet like Trevor told him to. Even threatened him if he didn't? This would be the perfect place to do it. To dispose of a body. They wouldn't, would they?

Twigs and dried pinecones cracked in the distance.

Someone else had arrived.

Twenty-Five

A car door slammed shut. The person hid in the dark shadows of the trees as they walked toward Jim and stopped. Neither of them said a word; only the night creatures chirped in the background.

"Hey, what took you so long?" Jim finally asked.

"I had things to do. What's it to you?" the male voice replied.

Then, there was silence.

"Listen, you have to stop sending out those videos. We didn't do anything wrong. We found her there."

"What the hell are you talking about? What videos?"

"Dude, don't play dumb; I know it was you. You were there."

"You can't prove it."

"Maybe not, but I know you're the one behind this. You're blackmailing Trevor to be your friend. You wrote that word on Mia's locker."

"The flying hell I did!" the male voice shouted. "I might have messed with Trevor, but I didn't write Slut on Mia's locker. So, get your damn facts straight, asshole!"

"What about Paige? She said you tried to get her to be your girlfriend," Jim said.

The unknown person let out a boisterous laugh that resonated across the hilltops.

My heart skipped a beat. "What a creep," I whispered. I still couldn't see the face of the person who had arrived. They were standing on the far side of the trees. Had he done that on purpose, or was it just a coincidence? I focused on the voice but couldn't identify the tone. The trees and night sounds altered the pitch.

"Yeah, well, it was worth a shot to try and get her to go out with me."

I was convinced it was Gavin because I remembered him standing by Paige's locker one morning. I tried to figure out what they were discussing. Videos? Did Gavin have footage of the girl being killed? If so, that meant he was there, just like Jim had mentioned. But how would Jim know Gavin was present unless he had attended camp too? And if he was there when it happened, did that imply he had killed her and was framing them? I wanted to uncover the truth, but I needed more information, and Jim wasn't asking the right questions.

They started shouting at each other. My eyes narrowed as Jim fell to the ground with a *thud*. Or had he been pushed? Part of me wanted to save him, but I couldn't reveal myself. I had to wait for the right moment, wanting to gather as much information as possible.

"Hey!" Trevor shouted as he leaped out from behind a tree. "You think your tough shit now just because you've been hanging out with me?"

The person turned sharply. "Oh, great. You brought your bodyguard to protect you. I thought you genuinely wanted to talk to me, perhaps apologize for your words over the summer, and become friends again, but now I see you're here to team up against me."

Jim stood up, brushing the dirt off his pants. "Me, apologize to you? You know, if you weren't such a wimp, I wouldn't have had to tell you to grow the hell up and get a life. You were too clingy all the time, like I was your boyfriend or something, wanting to hang out every damn second," Jim said. "Even when I had a girlfriend. God, it was like, get a freaking life already!"

"Screw you, Jim! You're all a bunch of damn losers! I knew I should've gone to the police and shown them the video. The three of you just stood there and didn't help her."

"Shut your pie hole, Gavin!" Paige yelled.

Well, he just confessed to videotaping them. I shook my head. *Dumbass.*

A burst of ugly laughter erupted from deep within Gavin. He howled, sending echoes ricocheting off the rugged cliffs surrounding us. “Oh, this is too good to be true. You’re here, too. I should have known you’d join their little outing. Do they make you feel all high and mighty, Paige?”

“I won’t let you ruin my life over something we didn’t do, so shut the hell up!” Paige said through clenched teeth, her voice deep like a frog. I had never seen her this feisty.

“Or what? Are you gonna tell your two mommies on me? Freaking dyke. If your life is ruined, it’s because of what you did, not me. If you want to cheat on your SATs, then you’re the one at fault, not me bitch.”

“Just stop!” Mia screamed.

“Oh, I should’ve known you’d be here too. What? The football champ can’t go anywhere without his suicidal girlfriend by his side. Better make sure you don’t have a razor on you. You might slice me with it, but then again, you couldn’t even kill yourself. You’re so pathetic, Mia.” He let out another laugh.

I couldn’t believe he had the guts to talk about Mia like that in front of Trevor.

“Shut it, or I will shut your mouth for you,” Trevor growled, stepping forward.

"I'm not scared of you. You think you're so tough, but you're just a boy whose father was killed by some lunatic, and your mother gets drunk all the freaking time because she doesn't want to live anymore. Perhaps she and Mia should meet up to find a better way to end their lives. Or maybe it's you, Trevor, they want to escape from. You know what? You all are just worthless pieces of shit, and I hope you all die from gonorrhea."

Gavin was such an ass. Maybe he deserved to be bullied. Listening to him talk, I'd bet his mouth had gotten him into trouble all those times he ended up in a locker.

In that second, Jim leaped through the air like a ninja. I couldn't see where he had landed, but I was positive he had been aiming for Gavin. Why did it have to be so dark out here?

Paige let out a piercing scream, making me slap a hand over my ears.

Then everything happened so fast like someone had hit the fast-forward button on the TV. Shadows merged. Trevor chased Gavin like a fly on shit. Then, another scream filled the air. It resonated close, then distant, before being engulfed by the surrounding darkness. The kind of fearful scream that pricked the tiny hairs on your arms as it crawled along your skin, inching up the back of your neck and sending tingles throughout every hair follicle on your scalp. I hid behind the tree stump, paralyzed with fear, placing a hand over my mouth to stifle a scream. My legs felt like Jell-O, and I used the tree to hold myself up, the rough bark digging into my palm. Then, complete silence filled the air around me.

I held my breath.

Listening.

No bullfrogs croaking or crickets chirping. Only the hollow sound of tranquility, waiting for something else to happen. Like a theatrical finale. Before the silence, a shrill sound came from deeper in the forest. A panicky shriek before one's death.

I gasped, my hand still pressed against my lips. A chill ran up my spine. "Oh, God, no!" The words tickled the delicate skin of my lips as they escaped my mouth.

Was that why they were out here? To kill him? Had he been killed? I wasn't sure, relying only on my ears to piece together what was happening. I used their voices to determine where they were standing. I had been out here for a while, considering how long it took me to walk to this spot. Outlines materialized in front of me—nothing more. Then they disappeared as a dark overcast rolled in, covering the moon. The only light I had left was now gone.

A crackling sound pricked at my ears.

Running.

Someone was running.

No, not just one person, but several.

Footsteps ricocheted all around me as tree branches snapped beneath sneakered feet. Not one but two car doors slammed shut, and an engine roared to life. Two glowing, round beams of light emerged in front of me. Trees of all shapes and sizes surrounded me like a big fat bully hovering over a small child, feeling scared and afraid.

Twigs crunched and popped, breaking into hundreds of pieces as the vehicle backed up, its lights now shining in my direction. I sank to the ground, shielding myself with the trunk of an old, hollow tree, hoping against hope that they hadn't seen me. My heart thrashed like a caged monkey.

I placed a hand over my mouth, suppressing a scream. It was an all-too-familiar scene from a horror movie where the girl hides from the killer just before he jumps out from behind a tree and murders her. They were unaware I was there. What would they do to me if they knew? I was now a witness.

I closed my eyes, hugged my body tightly, and waited for the car to drive away. The headlights disappeared, and darkness loomed over me once again. With trembling hands, I fished out my cell phone. It slipped from my grasp and fell to the ground. I patted around until I felt the rectangular shape beneath my fingers, scooping it up and tapping the flashlight icon at the bottom of the screen.

"Get it together, Kat. Everything is fine. Everything will be fine," I muttered, though I was full of it after everything I had heard and seen. The truth was, I had never been in a situation like this, not when someone might have been killed.

I took a breath and exhaled. Looking down at my hands, I clenched them into a fist. The tremors faded like a wisp of smoke from my grandfather's pipe. With one hand, I snatched the phone from my lap and grabbed the tree with the other, pulling myself up on unsteady legs. I stumbled toward the clearing, using the light from my cell phone to illuminate my path. I shone the light across the ground and at the trees but saw nothing. It would be difficult to notice anything in the dark, anyway. I should leave and come back tomorrow when I could take a better look around.

I turned and walked back the way I had come. My foot struck something. I shone the light on the ground in front of me. A shoe? Had one of them lost a shoe when they ran out of here? I wasn't sure. I knelt down to get a better look.

I inhaled sharply.

I knew exactly who the shoe belonged to. The distressed red stains gave it away. A spark of light flashed in front of me as I took a photo of the shoe lying on the ground. A respectable detective never handled objects at a crime scene. But was this a crime scene? There was no body—only a shoe. A boy's shoe. A boy that I knew. A boy who wore a shoe with red Slurpee stains.

I gasped for air, trying not to think of the worst.

My mind rewound. Only one car drove away. I shined the light around. There was something up ahead. Moving in that direction, I stopped, standing several feet back. The vehicle belonged to the same person as the shoe.

It belonged to Gavin.

Well, I knew it was him because Paige said his name, but now I was absolutely sure of it. I walked around the car, shining the light inside; no one was there. So, if he wasn't in the car, where was he? I scanned the area and spotted the cliff. Signs were posted everywhere, warning people to stay away from the edge.

Nausea filled my stomach as I swallowed the sour taste rising in my throat and walked to the far side. Darkness draped around me like a curtain closing at the end of a play. I didn't need to look to know it was a long drop to the bottom, where a person would lie crumbled and unrecognizable. I should leave and return tomorrow to look around in the daylight. But I won't leave. I can't leave. I need to know if he has fallen over the cliff.

My fingers wrapped around the small sapling, and I gave it a shake, silently praying that it would hold me as I leaned over the bluff. Dirt and rocks tumbled over the edge as I positioned my foot near the brink. It wasn't safe, so I stepped back.

I twisted my body to leave. A flash of light appeared and then vanished. I dashed over to the spot and reached into the bushes. Thorns scraped my arm as I pulled out a cell phone. First, a shoe, then a car, and now a cell phone. Where was the person who owned these items?

A faint whisper brushed against my ear. I paused, inhaling deeply and leaning my body toward the origin of the sound.

Blood pulsed in my eardrum.

Positive, I was hearing things now. I turned back around. The sound came again.

"Help me."

Twenty-Six

"Shit, shit, shit," I cursed. Dry leaves and pine needles crunched and snapped under my feet as I paced back and forth. I had to do something, but what? Clumps of darkness obscured the moon. I wouldn't, no, I couldn't see over the cliff to be one hundred percent sure that someone was down there. That Gavin had fallen over the edge of the cliff and was… Was what? Dying? Dead? He had called out for help, which meant he wasn't dead, right?

My hand flew to my mouth as I stifled a cry. My knees gave way, and I collapsed to the ground. I couldn't believe it. They had pushed him off the cliff to silence him.

Sitting on the hard ground covered in pinecones and dried twigs wasn't an option. I needed to stand up and figure out how to help him. If I couldn't climb down there to save him, I would have to call for help.

I lifted my phone, swiped up, and opened my contacts. If I called my dad, would he be furious with me? Would he punish me for being out in these woods at night, alone? For sneaking out of the house without telling him? I wondered what he would do when he found out that I had followed my classmates out here and witnessed what they had done. I wished I could see down to the bottom where the jagged rocks shaped the hillside, where someone could have fallen— or had they been pushed over the edge?

Pushed? My stomach churned. The worst thing I could do was vomit, and then they, the police, would know I was out here. Well, they wouldn't know it was me but that someone had been out here. I had seen TV shows where they could trace stomach contents back to a certain person. I wasn't sure how much of it was fictional, but it could be possible. It could be done.

As I stood back up, dizziness washed over me. I closed my eyes, allowing the fuzziness to fade away. The scream echoed in my mind. Images of Jim being thrown to the ground, followed by Trevor emerging from the shadows. Then everything merged together until that dreadful, chilling scream.

If the police showed up here, I wouldn't be able to explain what really happened because I wasn't sure myself. Parts of tonight didn't fit together like pieces of a puzzle.

My eyes fell back to the phone in my hand. There were no bars, which meant I had no reception out here in these woods. I was in a dead zone. But what did that mean, exactly?

I sucked in a deep breath, held it, then exhaled, allowing my chest to fall. *Stay calm, Kat. Don't let yourself get worked up over nothing, but it was for something, wasn't it? I needed to save Gavin.*

Then it occurred to me: Even if I called my dad, how would he get here? I had the car. I would have to go home and get my father, tell him everything. He would know what to do, and if Gavin fell over the cliff, my dad would save him. Yes, that was exactly what I needed to do.

I scanned the scenery. I had been pacing around the area and wasn't sure which path I had taken. Everything appeared unchanged in the dark, blending together in the deepening shadows. I spun around, scanning the woods. I wasn't certain which direction to take. Darkness enveloped the area around me. I looked up at the sky; thick, charcoal clouds obscured the moon, leaving me with no choice but to start walking.

I used my cell phone's flashlight to light my way as I trudged through the forest ahead of me. Minutes passed, though it felt like hours. I wasn't sure how long I had been walking when the light from my phone went out. I pressed the side button, but nothing happened.

"Freaking great," I muttered. My cell phone had died, leaving me without light and unable to call for help, even if

I had reception. *Worst of all, I think I'm lost out here.* I used to know these woods, but the truth is I knew them in daylight, not at night when you can't distinguish one tree from another.

A cool wind tousled my hair and tickled my nose. I shivered, wrapping my arms around myself for warmth, but it didn't help. I hadn't brought a jacket because it had been warmer these past few days, though I was in a hurry and didn't think to grab one. I hadn't been out at night to know how cool it could get. The best thing to do was to keep walking until I either came to a road or someone's home and could call for help.

My father was going to wake up and find his car missing, and then he would go into my room and find me missing, too. He'd start calling my cell phone, which was now dead, and begin to worry. My dad would find me; I was sure of this. He was a detective. He found people who were lost, right? Besides, wouldn't his police car have a tracker on it?

As I trudged through the woods, my mind replayed the events that had brought me here. I needed to figure out what really happened once I got out of here and back home. Suddenly, an idea sparked in my mind. Gavin's car was here. Why hadn't I searched for his car? Then, I would know which way to go, which would lead me back to my dad's car.

I turned around and began walking back in the direction I had come from. Maybe it was foolish, but I didn't have any other choice, really. I hadn't seen anything so far.

My legs ached from all the walking, and I needed to stop and rest against the tree. Though it was futile, I kept fiddling with my phone, hoping desperately that it had some battery life left. Unfortunately, it didn't, so I slipped it into my back pocket. A heaviness settled in my limbs as if they were filled with cement. I couldn't stay here; I needed to keep walking.

I stepped away from the tree. A branch snapped somewhere in front of me. I held my breath, listening intently as my eyes darted in every direction. From the corner of my eye, a light flickered, and then it vanished. Focusing, I waited and watched. Was someone out here? If so, who? Should I call out to them? My mind quickly screamed, *"No!"* It would be a bad idea since I didn't know who they were. Maybe a mass murderer? I wanted to laugh at myself.

Yes, Trevor's father was killed two years ago, but the guy had been caught, and as far as everyone knew, he was still in prison for the shooting. According to the news, there had been a brawl at the bar, during which the other guy pulled a gun and shot Trevor's dad in the chest three times, killing him instantly. So, no, the guy wasn't actually a mass murderer, and there wasn't one lurking in these woods now.

My mind did that sometimes, always coming up with absurd ideas that weren't true. But one thing's for sure: don't get drunk and anger someone. You never know what they might do or what weapon they could have.

There it was again, a flash of light, and then nothing. On, off, on, off. Then it struck me. I had found Gavin's phone earlier and dropped it on the ground.

A question plagued me. Should I go to the blinking light? But hadn't I heard branches breaking somewhere in front of me? Yes, I had, but that had been minutes ago, right? Besides, I was sure it was an animal, possibly a deer. Deer can sense people in the woods.

Well, I could stay here until daylight or follow the light and get the hell out of here. Without hesitation, I pushed away from the tree and headed straight for the phone that lay somewhere in front of me. I kept my eyes fixed forward in the exact spot where I'd seen the light that wasn't blinking now. It occurred to me that someone was probably calling the phone, which meant there had to be reception in that area. That was why it was flickering on and off. I raced to the place where I thought the cell had fallen. I paused and scanned the ground. Leaves crunched behind me, and then something hard struck the back of my skull. My body collapsed to the ground, and everything went black…

Part Two

To question the existence of life,
would be to question never living at all...

Quoted by: Donna M. Zadunajsky

Twenty-Seven

"Kat."

A warm voice whispered my name, but no one was there. My eyes fluttered beneath closed lids, searching. Where was I? Darkness surrounded me.

"Kat, can you hear me?" the voice asked.

I willed my eyes to open, but they felt heavy as though they were sewn shut.

I slept.

Twenty-Eight

A bright beam of light pricked my eyes as I opened them. I lifted my left hand to shield my eyes, feeling the tape pulling against my skin. I turned my head toward my arm as a sharp pain stabbed the back of my skull. Using my other arm, I reached a hand to my head, wincing in discomfort. Why was my head hurting so much? I squeezed my eyes shut, trying to recall what might have happened, but my mind drew a blank.

"Kat."

Was it the same voice I had heard before? A chair scraped across the floor, then something brushed against my arm. I opened my eyes; the room was a shade darker than it had been a minute ago. I moved my head slowly, trying not to inflict more pain on myself, and looked into Jim's eyes. What was he doing here in my bedroom? Hadn't we broken up? I forced myself to sit up, but the discomfort in my head screamed at me like a mother reprimanding her child.

"Hey, don't move, just lie there. I'll get the nurse."

Nurse? I asked. *Why would I need a nurse?* My eyes moved away from Jim and scanned the room. It had pale walls and fluorescent lights. A whiteboard with my name scribbled on it hung on the wall.

"Why am I in the hospital?" I croaked, rubbing my throat with my right hand as I swallowed. "How long have I been here?"

"Shh, don't speak. I'll get you some water."

I closed my eyes and opened them again. My mind was filled only with fog. I couldn't recall how I ended up in the hospital. The bed started to move as Jim pressed a button on the side, and I inclined to a sitting position.

"Here you go." He put the straw between my lips.

I took a few sips and then pushed the straw aside. My mouth felt like cotton. I ran my tongue over my dry, chapped lips. "Why am I in the hospital? What happened?"

"You don't remember?"

I started to shake my head, but then I stopped.

"They discovered you in the woods at Lemmon's Park. Someone struck you on the back of the head."

"That explains why my head hurts."

He nodded.

"Why was I out there?"

"No one knows why. They found your dad's car at Camp Wilson. We're all assuming you walked to Lemmon's Park."

"Who found me?"

He shook his head. "I don't know. Someone made an anonymous call to the police."

"So, I was alone in the woods?"

He averted his gaze from me.

My mind raced, searching for answers. Why was I in Lemmon's Park alone? Even stranger was that I had left my car a quarter of a mile away. Why had I done that? Why hadn't I just driven to the park? My head throbbed from all the thinking; it was too much. I couldn't remember anything.

"Hey, you're awake," a male voice called from across the room.

I turned toward the door just as the intercom chirped. My dad shut the door behind him, cutting off the noise. I smiled, feeling relief wash over me.

"How are you feeling?" he asked.

"Aside from my head feeling like it might explode, I'm alright. But I can't recall what happened."

He offered a tentative smile, running his hand through his hair.

My eyes scanned my father. His eyes were puffy and bloodshot. I was certain he hadn't been sleeping in the hospital with me. Or could it be something else keeping him awake?

"Your watch," I questioned.

"My watch?" My father looked at his wrist before lowering it again.

"You aren't wearing it."

His face lost all color. "Yeah, well, it's been missing since the break-in we had," my father said, averting his gaze from me.

"Oh." My gaze dropped to the white, crisp sheets draped over my body. *A break-in? Someone had broken into our house.*

"You'll remember when your concussion fades," my dad said, wiping a bead of sweat from his forehead.

I glanced over at Jim. Did he just flinch at my dad's words? I might be imagining things. But didn't we break up? Yet, he was here with me now, which meant he still cared about me, right? Yes, of course, he did. Why else would he be by my side? Unless we were back together? No, I was sure we weren't. I wouldn't forget something like that, would I?

"So, I spoke with the doctor, and they're going to keep you here for a couple more days to ensure that the swelling goes down and that there's no damage to your brain," my dad said.

I groaned.

"I'm sure Jim here will get whatever you need from school. I don't want you to get all worked up about falling behind in your classes," my dad smiled.

Yes, the Kat before her head injury would have freaked out if she missed school, but the Kat now couldn't care less. It was the last thing on my mind. All I wanted was to remember what had happened to me.

Twenty-Nine

Three days later, I climbed out of the car and walked into our house. Eva danced around the room, excited to see me; I knelt on the floor, still a little unsteady on my feet, probably from the pain medication the doctors had given me.

"Hey, pretty girl," I said to the dog. "I missed you so much." I kissed her head and scratched behind each ear. Eva tilted her head sideways. Her eyes closed, savoring the attention. I could swear she was smiling back at me as I did that.

"Come on, let's get you to bed so you can rest," my dad said.

"Ugh, haven't I rested enough?" I stood up, and a wave of lightheadedness washed over me. I stumbled off balance, grabbing the wall for support. I peeked out of the corner of my eye. My dad was staring at me.

"You were saying?"

I guess he saw me. "I just stood up too fast, that's all."

“Doctor’s orders. You can return to school next week; we’ll see how you feel.”

“I wasn’t thinking about school. I just hate lying in bed.”

“I know, but I’ll get you some books to read, and there’s always Netflix,” my dad said with a broad smile.

Yay, my mind grumbled. I wasn’t a big fan of TV, but I could rewatch Bones or CSI. I nodded in response and took small steps as I made my way down the hall to my room. I opened the door, flicked on the light, and screamed.

“What’s wrong?” my dad called out as he hurried down the hall. He stood next to me and looked into the room. A dead rat lay in the middle of the floor. He moved closer to the rodent and knelt down. “How the hell did this get in here?” He stood up and walked to the doorway. “I’ll be right back with a bag.”

My cell phone buzzed in my back pocket. I pulled it out to find a text from an unknown number. I tapped on the iMessage and read the message.

> **Unknown:** Mind your own business, or you’ll end up a dead rat.

My eyes shifted from my phone to the rat on the floor. How did they know I was here? That I had just seen the rat in my room? I stepped into the room and searched everywhere but found no hidden cameras. Maybe they were outside my bedroom window.

I crossed the room and peered outside but didn't see anything. I sat on the edge of my bed, my hands shaking. My dad came into the room with a plastic bag, disposing of the rat. I read the text again. Who sent this to me? But what frightened me the most was the fact that the person had been in my room, in my house. This had to be the same person who broke into our house last week.

Wait! How did I know that? I remembered something. Memories flashed in my mind like a slide projector. They left the camera on the back porch for me to find—the one I had set up to record the intruder. Mia's house. Then, the faces of Trevor, Paige, and Jim appeared in my thoughts. What did they have to do with all of this?

I wanted nothing more than to recall what had happened. Were they linked somehow? Yes, I was sure of it. Now, all I needed to do was figure out a way to spark more of my memories and the events that had put me in the hospital. Maybe I needed to go to where it all happened, but how was I going to get there? Driving wasn't a possibility; besides, my father wouldn't allow it. I was certain he wasn't going to leave my side anytime soon.

Maybe I could persuade Jim to take me. The moment I woke up in the hospital, he had been acting all weird, which told me something was going on. Had he been there when it happened? No, he said, I had been alone.

I placed a hand on the back of my head as a headache crept back in. I would let myself rest for now and then devise a plan to return to Lemmon's Park. There was something out there—clues to what had happened to me. I was certain of it.

Thirty

I opened my eyes and spotted Jim sitting across the room, staring out the bay window, oblivious to the world around him. Something felt off about him since I had woken up in the hospital days ago, almost as if he felt responsible for how I ended up there. It hadn't occurred to me until now that he could have been there in the woods that night. I hated not being able to remember anything. But if that were true, then it meant he flat-out lied to me, and I couldn't trust him.

Pushing myself up to a sitting position, I reached back, adjusted the pillow behind me, and leaned against it. I glanced at the clock beside the bed. It read 6:56 a.m. Where had yesterday gone? Had I really slept through the entire night? What time did Jim arrive?

"Hey, how are you feeling?" Jim asked.

"Good. I'm good."

"You're full of shit, Kat. You don't think I know when you're lying?" He shook his head, stood up, and walked to the end of the bed where he sat down.

That makes two of us. "How long have you been here?"

"Not long. About ten minutes." He placed a hand on my foot, which was covered by the thick duvet. We looked at each other, just like we used to. "You know, I still want to understand why you broke up with me. Did I do something to hurt you? Did I say something wrong?"

His words squeezed at my heart. Should I be honest with him? I really didn't have a reason not to. I broke his heart to protect myself. But maybe I had jumped the gun. I loved him, and he still loved and cared for me. Why else would he be here? Why couldn't we be together? It was a question I had asked myself since I ended it with him.

"Kat," he persisted.

I closed my eyes, took a deep breath, and loosened the knot around my heart. "When my mom got sick, I... I had a really hard time accepting that I wouldn't see her again."

His eyes glistened with tears as he listened to me speak. Was he on the verge of crying?

"The more time I spent with my mom and watched her slip away from me, the more I hurt. The more of myself I lost. I loved her so much. I love you so much. That's why I had to push you away." I wiped a tear from my eye. "I didn't want that day to come when you decided you didn't want me anymore, that you would leave one day, and I would be heartbroken all over again."

"So, you thought that leaving me would save you from getting hurt?"

I winced. Now that I heard the words out loud, it did seem foolish.

"Aren't you hurting now?"

Oh, God, yes. But could I tell him that? Would it make a difference if he knew I had made a mistake? I regretted shoving him aside to protect myself from something I never expected. The future was uncertain. Not just for me but for everyone. I had no idea what my life would bring.

"You said you still love me?"

My eyes widened. Had I really said those words out loud? Heat surged from my stomach to my face, flushing my cheeks. This was what I wanted, right? I missed him and longed to be with him so much, but what about my heart? Shouldn't I protect it from breaking? My mother's words echoed in my head. *"Katherine, you must keep living your life after I'm gone. Be happy. Find that special someone and love them with all your heart. I'll always be watching over you. You'll always be my bumblebee."*

"Kat."

I snapped out of my thoughts and looked up into his bluish-green eyes—eyes that reminded me of the ocean in the tropics of Jamaica. "Yes, I still love you, Jim Covinski. I always have and always will." My heart fluttered as the words spilled out of my mouth. A slow smile spread across my face. Lost in my own thoughts, I hadn't noticed that Jim was now inches from my face. From my lips. He kissed me—a kiss that deepened the longer we lingered. My body felt as if it were floating on a cloud.

He pulled away slowly, his eyes still half-closed. "Wow!" he whispered, staring into my eyes.

Joyful tears slid down my face as I grinned, feeling carefree. My heart released the chains I had wrapped tightly around it. Shouldn't I feel guilty for wanting to be with him? For finally letting go and loving again? For wanting to be loved. What kind of life would I have if I locked myself away from love? I was seventeen; I had an entire life ahead of me. I remembered the words my mom had spoken just minutes before she passed away. She wouldn't want me to waste another second locked away in my room, away from the life that continued outside the walls of this house.

"So, Katherine, will you be my girl again?"

"Katherine?" I questioned. He had never called me Katherine; only my parents did.

"Yeah, Jimmy, I'll be your girl again." We both laughed, and he kissed me over and over.

"This time, we talk. No secrets, alright?"

I nodded. "Alright. If there are no secrets, then I have a few questions I need answers to."

He observed me for a moment, then replied, "Sure, go ahead and ask."

I could tell by the crease lines on his forehead that he was skeptical. I stared at him for a few seconds, then spoke. "Since school started last week, you and Paige weren't a couple? Aren't a couple?"

He howled, his laughter echoing around the room. "Hell, no! Why would you think Paige and I were a couple?"

"Ever since school started last week, you and she have been spending time together."

He shook his head and then stopped.

"Along with Trevor and Mia," I said. He swallowed, rubbing the back of his neck. "And we can't forget Gavin."

The moment I said his name, a flash came back to me: the woods. They were all in the woods that night. Jim and Gavin were arguing about something, then Trevor appeared out of nowhere. Paige and Mia's voices filled the air. Why were they all out there? I saw headlights, then Trevor's car peeling out of the woods, leaving me alone. I was hiding in the woods, but why? How did I end up there?

There was something else. Someone else.

Where was Gavin?

Thirty-One

"I... I can't tell you," Jim replied.

"We just agreed no more secrets."

"I just can't."

"Why?"

"It's bigger than us, Kat. It will annihilate everything. It will ruin lives."

His expression faltered as he stood up from the bed. Was he going to leave now? I reached for his hand, and he let me take it. "Talk to me. Maybe I can help. Does it have anything to do with that girl they found dead in the woods near Camp Wilson?"

He jumped back as though he had seen a snake; his hand slipped from my grip.

"What are you talking about?"

"Hello, it was in the newspaper. I saw it on the second day of school."

"Newspaper?"

"Yes, the newspaper, Jim." *What was wrong with him? Did I really have to spell it out for him?* "You do know what a newspaper is, right?"

"Kat, I don't know how to say this, but there isn't a dead girl."

"What? Yes, there is. The police found her last week. I'll prove it." I threw off the blankets and stood up, rushing toward the kitchen. I went straight to the recycling bin under the kitchen sink, only to find it empty. Maybe my dad had taken it outside with the rest? I threw open the back door and marched down the stairs to the side of the garage. Once there, I lifted the lid and looked inside. It was empty, too.

"Kat, what are you doing?" Jim shouted from the steps on the back porch.

The lid slipped from my hand and banged shut. Memories flooded my mind as I remembered sitting at the kitchen table with my dad. I recalled the article stating that a girl was found stabbed to death in Lemmon's Park. My father had said there were no suspects, no witnesses, and no weapon.

"Kat."

The world spun in circles, and my head became dizzy. My vision blurred, and my body fell backward.

"Kat!" Jim screamed.

Something soft brushed against my cheek. I turned and looked up at Jim, who was kneeling beside me. I was on the ground looking up at him.

"Are you okay?"

Shaking my head, I felt far from okay. Confusion swirled in my mind like a tornado. "Jim, I swear I read an article last week about a girl found dead in the woods. But you're telling me there wasn't a girl? It doesn't make sense."

His Adam's apple bobbed as he swallowed. He appeared anxious about something.

"Maybe everything got mixed up in your mind, and you think you saw it. That you read about it. Maybe you heard your father talking to someone about a case last night or even early this morning. It's possible, you know. Voices can travel through walls."

True, but why did I still believe he was lying to me? His posture and facial expressions suggested otherwise. I looked away and then back at his face, studying the lines on his forehead as he gazed at me with concern. He thinks I'm losing my mind. The blow to my head caused me to believe something that never happened. Something that wasn't factual. Yet it all felt real to me. How could I have made something like that up? Why would I?

Jim led me back inside the house and down the hall to my bed. I stared at the floor beneath my bare feet, wiggling my toes into the soft, fuzzy carpet. I shook my head as if to jostle the details back into place, but it was no use. Maybe Jim was right, and I had made up the whole thing.

"Drink this and then lie down for a while," Jim said, handing me a glass.

When did he leave the room? I couldn't recall a glass next to my bed. Nodding my head, I gulped down the entire glass of water and handed it back to him.

He set the pillow flat and raised my legs onto the bed, draping the blankets over my body.

"You need to get some sleep. You're pushing yourself too hard and getting all worked up over nothing."

My eyelids grew heavy. I had pushed myself too hard, running to the kitchen and then outside to check the recycling can. "Yeah," I yawned, covering my mouth with a hand. My eyes closed, and I fell fast asleep.

~

Later, when I woke up, I found myself drenched in sweat. I didn't remember having a nightmare, nor did it feel hot in the room. I placed the back of my hand against my forehead like my mom used to do. It was cool and clammy, but I had no fever.

I peeled back the blanket and the sheet that clung to my body before sitting up. My head felt heavy, swimming with lightheadedness, so I laid back down. The moment my head hit the pillow, pain shot through the base of my skull toward my eyes. In my grogginess, I had forgotten about the blow to my head.

I closed my eyes. Images flashed through my mind. I needed to piece everything together, but the puzzle had too many missing pieces.

My body jolted upright. My eyes scanned the room. Why was I hearing bullfrogs croaking? My head whipped to the left at the sound of crickets chirping. Where was that sound coming from? I closed my eyes. I was standing in the woods.

Voices.

I heard several voices in front of me, but I couldn't see them—only listen. It was too dark. With my eyes still closed, kneeling beside a tree, I felt the rough bark against my palm. I inhaled the scent of pine and decomposing leaves. I was hiding somewhere in the woods. Was a memory returning to me? Tree branches snapped under car tires.

Then footsteps.

Jim's voice, followed by Gavin's. They were arguing about something. My memories grew hazy. What were they doing out there? What happened that night? What was I missing?

Thirty-Two

That was it.

I needed to return to Lemmon's Park and search around. I had to understand what I witnessed that got me knocked unconscious and what I might have heard that night. Because why else would someone try to kill me? Did someone really try to kill me? I hadn't considered that before. The only motive would be to cover up something they did. That was the answer I needed to my question. I had to uncover the truth. I needed to determine if Jim was honest about the girl. Perhaps I already knew, and that was why someone had struck me on the head. I must remember what happened.

I stepped into the hall wearing sweatpants and a 3 Doors Down T-shirt. It was my mom's favorite band and the first real concert she said she'd attended with an old boyfriend before meeting my dad. They had opened for Creed in Toledo, Ohio, in 2000. She once mentioned that after hearing their music, she was hooked for life. Wearing some of her clothes made me feel closer to her. It empowered me and made me feel fearless.

I walked into the empty kitchen. Glancing at the clock on the microwave, I saw that it was a little past three in the afternoon. This meant my dad was still at work, at least until six.

My eyes scanned the room. A set of keys hung on the wall. I wasn't sure why I hadn't thought about it before. My dad never got rid of my mom's car. Was he saving it for graduation day? But why hadn't he just given it to me when I got my driver's license? Well, I would have to ask him later. Right now, I needed to get to Lemmon's Park before dark.

I slipped on my tennis shoes, pulled on my jacket, and grabbed the keys from the hook. With one hand on the doorknob, I opened the garage door and stepped into the darkness. Feeling along the wall, I pressed the button, and light illuminated the cement floor. The chain clanked as it lifted the garage door. There, in front of me, under a blue cloth, was my mom's car.

With no time to waste, I dashed down the steps and began to pull the cover off the car, surprised that no dust was swirling around me. The car had been sitting here and undriven for over half the year, hadn't it? Yet there was no dirt settled on it. Well, as much as I wanted to unravel the mystery behind it, I didn't have the time. I just hoped the car would start, not remembering my father ever taking it out of the garage.

I jogged around to the driver's side, opened the door, and slipped in behind the wheel. The aroma of sweetness filled my nostrils. The fragrance of peonies lingered in the air as if my mom were sitting next to me. I closed my eyes and inhaled the sweet scent, recalling how she always made a drive into town feel like an exciting road trip to a different place.

I smiled and opened my eyes. In front of me was the trinket I had made for her when I was seven, still hanging from the rearview mirror. As much as I wanted to sit here and reminisce about my mom and all the times we drove together in this car, I had to put my memories aside for another time.

I wiped away the tears streaming down my cheeks and turned the key in the ignition. A burst of laughter escaped me when the car roared to life. Well, it was now or never. I shifted the car into reverse and slowly backed out of the garage. If my calculations were right, it would take me fifteen to twenty minutes to get there.

~

I pulled onto the gravel road and stopped. This was it. Hopefully, I would discover what I wasn't remembering and unravel the mystery of the dead girl and Gavin.

Minutes later, I parked the car and gazed out the windshield. The view was stunning from where I sat, but I wasn't there to enjoy the scenery. I opened the driver's door and stepped out. Leaning against the car, I shut my eyes, recalling more of the events that had taken place that night.

There was arguing, followed by a scream, as if someone were falling. I opened my eyes, searching for the cliff. There it was, ahead of me. I swallowed and took a step forward until I stood two feet from the edge. An image flashed in my mind: it was me that night, peering over the cliff, searching for something—but what? It was dark, and I was convinced it was the same night I'd been out here. The same night I was struck over the head.

Wrapping my arm around the tree, I leaned forward. Below me were only jagged rocks. No body. Did I really think there would be? It had been at least four days. Surely, the police would have checked the area. *Not if they didn't know what had happened out here,* my mind quipped.

Reflecting on that night, I was certain I had heard a scream. It didn't seem like anyone had fallen over the cliff, but it was a long way down to the bottom. Although it was possible that I had been mistaken since I hadn't seen anything, only heard that horrifying scream, Gavin hadn't fallen to his death.

As I stepped back from the edge, my shoe slipped, sending me down. My hip struck the ground hard. I yelped, my heart racing as my life flashed before my eyes.

"Come on, Kat. This is not how you're supposed to die." In those brief seconds, I contemplated what it would be like to be with my mom again, if, in fact, that's how things worked after we died. I didn't know. I don't believe anyone really knew what happens to a person when they die.

Rocks tumbled over the edge as I clung tightly to the sapling, pulling myself back from the brink, thankful that I hadn't fallen over the cliff. Once I was far enough away, I wiped the sweat from my brow with a shaky hand. I had to pause for a few seconds because I was sure I couldn't stand. My body trembled with fear.

My eyes scanned the scenery. I remembered kneeling behind a large stump when headlights appeared. After the car drove away, I left the tree and walked to the spot where I was sitting now. I got to my feet and turned in a circle, following my memory to the area where I had found a shoe.

Gavin's shoe.

The shoe with red Slurpee stains on it because Trevor spilled Jim's drink in the school hall.

I spun around in circles but didn't see a shoe anywhere. Had the police found the shoe and taken it? I placed my thumbnail between my teeth and paced back and forth. Then I stopped and snapped my fingers. Yes, of course. I recalled taking a picture as proof. I pulled my cell phone from my front pocket, thankful it hadn't fallen out when I fell, and opened my photo app. I tapped on the album and scrolled to the bottom. The most recent pictures were of my grandparents in Florida.

No shoe.

"What the hell!" I murmured. I kept searching my phone, but there was nothing. Not even the pictures I had taken of Trevor in the parking lot. Had someone accessed my phone and erased them? Deleted the photos so I wouldn't have proof? Proof of what, I wasn't sure yet.

Jim?

Jim had been with me the whole time since I woke up in the hospital. He must have been the one who got rid of the photos. Was he also the one who broke into my home? Did he leave the camera for me to find? And if so, had he lied about the article I thought I'd seen last week? But why would he do something like that? He claimed he loved me, or was that all a lie, too? My mind was a jumbled mess. Part of me wondered if a crime had been committed, and if so, did I have evidence of it? The evidence I no longer possessed.

Was Jim's plan all along to break into my home and steal whatever my dad had related to the case, as well as erase the photos I had taken? But the question that bothered me the most was whether he killed that girl and possibly Gavin.

Thirty-Three

My body sank to the ground, exhausted by everything that had happened. First, my mom died; then, I broke up with Jim. Instead of mourning both losses, I had sealed off my heart to prevent further damage.

Tears streamed down my face, and I didn't stop them. I needed to let out all the hurt in order to heal. What came next, I didn't know, but I couldn't hold the pain in any longer. I sat there on the ground without moving, not wanting to do much of anything. What was the point? The ones I loved were only out to hurt me.

I was here because of them. Actually, it was because of me. If I had walked away and not cared about the things going on around me that didn't even involve me, I wouldn't be sitting in these woods like I am right now. I wouldn't have been out here that night and wouldn't have ended up in the hospital. I could have died; then what? My father would not have known. He would have been alone, all because I had to play detective. I should have listened to Mia when she said to stay out of it, that it didn't concern me.

My sadness turned to anger. I stood up and dusted off my jeans. I would walk to my car, get behind the wheel, and drive straight home. No looking back. I no longer cared about what they did. In fact, I would tell Jim we couldn't be together because I didn't trust him. If he couldn't tell me the truth, then we were done. A Taylor Swift song, "*We Are Never Ever Getting Back Together,*" played in my head.

A sudden lightness washed over me. Why hadn't I done this sooner? Letting go of the irrational thoughts from deep within, I felt nearly one hundred percent better. Okay, it's ninety percent better.

I took a deep, much-needed breath to clear my lungs and mind. A whiff of smoke entered my nose. Was someone camping in these woods? Signs were posted all over, indicating that camping was not allowed, especially campfires. Didn't they realize how dangerous it was to start a fire in the woods?

Turning, I walked back toward the cliff, this time cautious of the dirt and stones near the edge. I scanned high and low for any signs of smoke but found none. Taking another deep breath, the scent of burning wood tickled the hairs in my nose. Without hesitation, I trudged through the forest, searching for the camper.

Who was I kidding? I loved playing the role of a detective. Sure, it got me into a few mishaps, but I always came out fine. I had never been caught off guard and hit over the head until recently. It was dark that night, and I hadn't heard anyone approach from behind. A branch had snapped, but I thought it was just a deer walking through the woods. Well, I'm fine now. There's no point in scolding myself for something that's already happened—something I couldn't change. It's in the past now. I needed to focus on finding the person who had built the fire.

Time slipped away like rushing water in a river. I glanced around. A splintered picnic table sat to my left, the same one I had seen the night I followed Trevor, Mia, Jim, and Paige. In front of me were cabins. I was at Camp Wilson.

Although I still believed a body had been found there, there was no sign of caution tape strung from any of the trees. I couldn't recall seeing any last week either, but I hadn't been looking.

I kept walking until I stood outside the cabin with wisps of smoke rising from the chimney. My senses indicated there had been a lot of smoke, but I had been walking for a while. The fire might have gone out. I looked for a vehicle but found none. If the person didn't drive here, how did they get here? Did they walk? From town?

The boards creaked under my weight as I climbed up the two steps of the wooden porch. I paused and listened. Logs crackled inside the cabin. Someone was definitely here. I had no idea what I was about to walk into. My stomach twisted into a knot.

I looked over my shoulder. There was no one there. The tension in my shoulders and neck faded away.

I was safe.

There was nothing to worry about. At least, not until I came face-to-face with whoever was inside.

"This is a bad idea," I mumbled under my breath. I reached out, grabbed the cold metal knob, and turned it.

Thirty-Four

The hinges creaked as I pushed the door open. I glanced over my shoulder. Leaves skittered in the wind behind me, sending chills of fear up and down my spine. I turned back around, hurried inside, and closed the door. Would I always feel the fear of someone sneaking up behind me after what had happened? Even if I don't remember being knocked out, it made me more alert.

The warmth in the room embraced me, making me almost comfy. I scanned the room. A glass half-full sat on the coffee table, and a blanket lay crumpled in a ball on the sofa cushion. The camp counselor may have left those items there, but that wouldn't explain the fire burning.

My eyes automatically fell on the fireplace to my left. Bright red and orange embers nestled in the ashes beneath the iron grate, still giving off a significant amount of heat, likely because the room had been sealed tight with no one coming in or out of the cabin. Seeing the fire for the first time, I was certain I hadn't heard wood crackling when I stood outside. It might have been the forest and its many critters roaming around breaking branches, or it could have just been my imagination.

To my right was a small kitchenette. I turned and headed in that direction. Someone had stacked dirty dishes in the sink with weeks of dried food on them, except for one. Using the sleeve of my jacket, I lifted the plate sitting on top. It wasn't baked-on like the rest of the dishes, which meant someone had been here recently. *Or is here now,* my mind suggested.

I put the dirty plate back in the sink and walked out of the kitchen. I stopped in front of a closed door, which I was sure was the bedroom. To the left of me stood the bathroom, with its white porcelain toilet glimmering back at me. Light beamed in through the small window beside the toilet.

I had two choices. One, I could step away from the door and walk out of the cabin. I could head back through the woods, get into my car, and drive away, never to return to this place again. I could pretend none of this ever happened. I would drive home, crawl beneath the comfort of my blankets, and fall asleep. I would wipe my hands of everything I had learned in the past week and not look back but move forward with my life with Jim. I would learn to trust him again and forget all that had happened. I could be happy. No, I would be happy.

I could either walk through the door in front of me and see who or what was on the other side. What would come next, I didn't know. Once I found out what was behind this door, I would decide what to do. I could still walk away and go home; that choice would be mine.

Without wasting another second, I reached out my hand and turned the knob. The door wouldn't budge. I gave it a forceful push, pressing my body against it, determined to get inside. The door swung open, stirring up dust that coated the wooden floor. I coughed as the particles entered my mouth, then gagged as I inhaled the odor trapped in the room. The stench I had just released lingered.

I stepped out of the room, hoping to breathe in some fresh air, but the smell lingered and followed me. Turning, I sprinted to the door and flung it open. A rush of cool air hit me in the face, and I inhaled a lungful of pine-scented air. Bending over with my hands on my knees, I breathed in and out until I couldn't smell anything but the surrounding forest.

I stood and turned back around, facing the open door. There was no way I was leaving now, no matter what horrific thing lay dead inside that room. I needed to know. I rushed back inside the cabin and paused outside the bedroom again. I rolled my shoulders back as if preparing for a fight. The stench of death still lingered in the air. I covered my nose and mouth with my jacket and stepped inside the room.

Curtains draped over the windows, allowing in minimal light. My eyes took a moment to adjust to the darkness. My body stiffened.

The quilt clung to the shape of a body lying beneath it. I couldn't tell who or what it was, whether it was a male or female, but I was certain it was human. And I was certain they weren't sleeping.

My knees began to buckle, so I placed my hand on the brass footrail to stabilize myself. I inched alongside the bed, stopping in front of the nightstand beside it. The person didn't move, which only confirmed my theory that they weren't alive. Besides, the entrance I had made a few minutes ago would have surely awakened them.

A beige blanket concealed the person's head. With the fabric of my jacket still covering my nose and mouth, I took a few breaths, inhaling the scent of detergent from the fabric of my clothes. Then, I reached out with a trembling hand and pulled the cover back from their head.

The fabric of the bedspread slipped through my fingers. I staggered backward from the bed, gasping as my back pressed firmly against the wall, startling me. My hand flew to my mouth.

"Oh, my God," I whimpered.

Tears brimmed in my eyes and raced down my face, falling to the floor. "Oh, my God. Oh, my God," I kept repeating as I shook my head in disbelief. I didn't want to accept what I was seeing, but there was no denying the truth. The person was, in fact, dead beyond saving. But the worst part was that I knew the person.

My mind automatically replayed every single scene from the past week until I found myself back in this room, staring at the body on the bed. I didn't know how the body got here, and it didn't matter. What mattered now was that I needed to call my dad and tell him what I'd discovered. He needed to come out here. He needed to get me out of here and take me home. Why hadn't I stayed home?

Nausea washed over me. I rushed out of the room and moved down the two steps. Once outside, I put my hands on my knees. I hadn't eaten anything recently, so I wasn't surprised when nothing came up. I reached into my front pocket and pulled out my cell phone.

Thirty-Five

Sirens grew louder as the emergency vehicles bounced up the winding driveway. The constant wailing buzzed in my head. Why were they so loud? My hands pressed firmly over my ears, blocking out the noise and causing my head to swirl with emotions I didn't understand and couldn't explain to anyone, even if I had to.

I sat on the steps outside the cabin, my head lowered to my bent knees. Every inch of my body shook, and my stomach felt sour. The ambulance stopped in front of the sign that read, "Welcome to Camp Wilson." I remained seated on the wooden steps outside the cabin where I had discovered the dead body of Paige Ziel.

Who could have done this to her? Trevor? Jim? I wouldn't be able to handle it if Jim had done this to Paige. Jim didn't have an angry side to him. I didn't want to believe it could've been Mia. But if it wasn't any of them, then who? Did that mean there was a murderer in this town?

I replayed that night once more in my mind, or at least what I could recall. I had assumed the four of them had fled the area, but maybe Paige hadn't? She wasn't anywhere visible or audible when I searched the area. So, how and when did she end up here at the cabin? And where had Gavin gone? Had he fallen over the cliff and somehow gotten himself back up the mountain? There were still a few things I didn't know, like where his car was. Did someone take his cell phone? Was he the one who knocked me out? All good questions I needed to find answers to. Maybe then it would lead to whoever had done this to Paige.

"Katherine," my dad shouted as he jogged over to me.

I stood and stumbled to the ground, my knees weak. Tears spilled from my eyes as he lifted my trembling body. I fell into his strong arms, and my tough ego vanished as I wept like a child. I didn't even care anymore. I had held my pain in for too long, and now it burst from every pore.

"Oh, my poor Katherine."

"Dad, I… I'm sorry. I'm so sorry."

"For what?" He stepped back, cupping my face in his hands.

"I know I shouldn't have come out here by myself. I needed to find out some things—clues about who might have hurt me."

"But here?" he asked. "You weren't attacked here, Katherine."

"I know, it was that way," I said, pointing behind me toward Lemmon's Park. "I was retracing my steps from that night when I smelled smoke, so I followed the scent that led me here." I wiped the snot from my nose with the back of my hand.

He nodded. "I understand that you want to solve this mystery, but Katherine, you can't be out here alone. What if something happened to you again? Did you let anyone know you were out here?"

I shook my head.

"Don't you remember a few days ago? You have to stop doing this before..."

"Hey, Boss, you might want to check this out," said an officer standing outside the cabin door.

My breath caught in my throat. *Had they found something? Something I had overlooked?* My heart raced, waiting to hear what they had uncovered, but the officer remained silent.

"Stay here; I need to see what they found," my father said.

He stepped around me and darted up the steps. I waited a few seconds and then followed him inside. He entered the room where Paige's lifeless body lay. There was no way I was going back in there. Instead, I stood with my back against the wall outside the bedroom, listening.

"Holy hell!" my father muttered.

"Boss, are you okay?"

"Yeah, yeah. I'm fine; it's just… I wasn't expecting this." He coughed and cleared his throat. "Could someone please open a window in here?"

"Yes, Boss."

"Okay, what did you find?" my dad finally asked.

I imagined my dad standing tall, puffing out his chest, eager to appear superior to his men and the others in the room.

"It seems like someone choked her. Do you see the discoloration around her neck here?" the female medical examiner said, "It probably happened days ago, but I can't be certain until I get her in the morgue and perform a full examination. The lighting isn't very good in here."

"What about her head?" my dad asked.

"It may be consistent with a fall, which would explain the cuts and scrapes on her face, arms, and legs. In my opinion, it looks like she was dragged."

Dragged? I repeated in my head. *I had paid little attention when I walked here. If someone had dragged a person, it would have flattened the dirt, creating a path. Sticks and debris would have been gathered from the body being towed. Of course, the killer could have taken another route to get here. Then I recalled that Gavin's car was missing from the scene. That brought me back to the question at hand: where was Gavin? Did Gavin do this?*

"What about that?" My father's voice interrupted my thoughts.

"It's a compound fracture of the tibia. That could explain how she lost so much blood. She never tied off the area to help stop the bleeding. Then again, the blow to the head didn't help her situation either," the examiner cleared her throat. "This girl definitely died here. No doubt about that. There's no way she got here on her own, but… but I can't be certain. Women are much stronger these days, you know."

I could sense the medical examiner smiling at her words, proud to be a woman herself. As the words sank in, my hand instinctively touched the back of my head.

Was Paige's attacker the same person who hit me in the head? If so, that meant whoever did this was still out there. Had they been watching me all along? Are they watching me now?

"So, how long do you think she's been here? I don't remember any missing person reports coming into the station recently?" my dad asked.

"As I mentioned earlier, I would say a couple of days. The temperature of the liver indicates two days, possibly three. I won't know for sure until I perform an autopsy." the examiner said. "I will reach out to the forensic pathologist as I head to the morgue."

My stomach flipped as my mind envisioned the scene of Paige's lifeless body in the morgue, resting on the cold metal examining table. I had seen many shows—I shut my eyes. I didn't want to dwell on that. I couldn't bear to think about Paige's perfectly sculpted body being sliced open like a piece of meat.

"Do you think it's connected to the girl we discovered out here a few weeks ago?" the officer asked.

"I don't know. That's why we need to take as many pictures as possible in every room. Fingerprint everything. If it's the same person, there will be a match. We need to catch this person before they kill again," my dad said. "I also want a few men out in the woods searching from here to Lemmon's Park."

"What are we searching for, Boss?"

"Whatever doesn't belong in the forest, Officer Rifkin," my dad said, his tone laced with mild irritation. "Look for torn clothing that matches what the victim was wearing. Maybe the person who did this left some evidence behind for us to find—something, anything we can use to catch them."

"Absolutely, Boss," Officer Rifkin replied.

"I told you, it's Detective Palmer out in the field, not Boss."

"Yeah, right? Sorry, Boss; I mean Detective Palmer."

The floorboards creaked as heavy boots approached the bedroom door. I rushed out the front door and glanced over my shoulder, relieved that no one saw me. It would upset my father if he discovered I was eavesdropping on the conversation.

Once outside, I stood several feet away from the steps, waiting for my dad to come out and tell me to go home, assuring me that I would see him later. I was certain it wouldn't be until late at night.

"Katherine," my dad called out. I'm going to have Officer Rifkin come here to take you home."

"What about my car?"

His head tilted to the side as his eyes narrowed at mine. "Your car?" he asked. "Since when do you have a car?"

"Well, it's not exactly my car yet," I smirked. "I, um… I borrowed mom's car to get here."

The color drained from his face. His eyes shifted away from mine and scanned the surroundings. "I don't see it."

"That's because it's at Lemmon's Park. I walked here from there."

"You what!?" his voice rose.

"I told you I smelled smoke, and I followed it here."

"Yeah, but you didn't mention anything about being in Lemmon's Park."

"Dad!" I snapped. "What's the big deal? I told you I was retracing my steps. I guess if you paid more attention to what I say half the time, you'd know." My heart sank, and tears brimmed in my eyes again. *Don't cry, don't cry,* my mind urged. *God, why did I have to say that out loud?*

"Katherine..." he paused, searching for the right words. "Look, I don't want you to get hurt, okay? Two kids have already died, and I don't want you to be next. Why didn't you bring Jim with you? At least you wouldn't have been alone."

I wasn't sure I could trust him at that moment, which was what I wanted to say to my dad. "He was busy; besides, I can take care of myself."

"Yeah, we know you think you can, but look what happened a few days ago." He took a deep breath and sighed. "You're all I have left, Katherine. I don't want to lose you too."

"Oh, Dad," I said, moving closer and wrapping my arms around his waist, pulling him in tight. "You won't. I promise."

"Okay," he said, though he didn't sound convincing. "I'll have Officer Rifkin take you to your mom's car, and then you should head straight home, understood?"

"Yes, Dad."

Thirty-Six

My mind went stir-crazy as the days slipped away. I had replayed the scene multiple times in my head, trying to piece together the puzzle, but I was still missing something. Why had they killed Paige? Did she know something? Something they didn't want the world to know.

"What am I missing? Jim said there was no girl found, but I swear I saw an article about her," I muttered aloud as I paced the floor in my bedroom. "Why would he lie to me?" *Then I remembered the officer at the cabin mentioning whether it was connected to the other girl, which meant Jim lied to me.*

A car door slammed, and I looked out my bedroom window toward the driveway. Nope, my dad wasn't home from work. I was about to turn away when my eyes caught sight of a police cruiser parked across the street in front of Mia's house. Had something happened? Should I go over there to make sure everything was okay? After last week, I was a little afraid to go back inside their house again, but I had to know what was going on.

I grabbed my phone to text Mia when an officer walked out of the house with Mia beside him. Her arms were wrapped across her chest, and there were no handcuffs on her wrists. This meant she wasn't under arrest, right? Then why were the police taking her away? Had something happened to her family? Was there an accident? Could it be related to Paige or Gavin? I didn't know, but I was determined to find out.

I grabbed the keys to my mom's car and headed out the door. After I convinced my dad to let me have the car, he finally broke down and gave me the keys.

"Dad, there's no reason for Mom's car to be sitting in the garage when I need a vehicle to drive," I suggested.

"I just... I mean..." he stammered.

"What is it, Dad? Tell me."

He exhaled deeply. "It's all I have left of her."

The words pierced my heart like a sharp knife. "Dad," I whispered. "We're not getting rid of the car. I'll keep it. Mom would want me to."

He smiled. "Yes, she would want you to have it, and I want you to have it too."

He handed me the keys, and I gave him a long hug, kissing him on the cheek. I jumped up and down, squealing like I had won the lottery. I no longer had to take the awful bus to school.

"Be careful and no speeding!"

"I know, Dad. I promise I'll be careful. You don't need to worry about me."

"That's something I'll always do, Katherine Ann."

And that was that. I had convinced him to let me have the car.

I waited a few seconds, then backed out of the driveway and slipped in behind them as they drove into town.

I parked the car and watched the officer escort Mia from the cruiser to the building. I needed to know what was happening, so I dashed toward the building. Once inside, I greeted Officer Grady, who was sitting behind the reception desk. She was the only officer with a southern twang working here. It wasn't unusual, just something you didn't often hear in the North. She was a Southern belle through and through. I wasn't sure what made her move up north.

I turned left and saw Mia as the officer led her into one of the interrogation rooms. I hurried down the hall, glancing over my shoulder before slipping into the observation room next to the one Mia was in.

On the wall was a two-way mirror, and to my surprise, Trevor was in the room on the other side. Nothing like 'killing two birds with one stone,' as they say. Then it hit me.

If Mia and Trevor were here, did that mean Jim had to be here too? That would make sense. They were in the woods that night, but how would the police know that? And why wasn't I being questioned as well?

"Please have a seat, and someone will be with you shortly," the officer's voice echoed through the speaker.

Mia pressed her elbows into her sides, making herself smaller. Clearly, she was scared, but I wondered why one of her parents hadn't come with her. At seventeen, Mia would typically need a parent present for questioning unless she wasn't under arrest, as I had already assumed. The police have every right to question a minor without a parent or guardian present, though a parent can still be there if the minor wants them. I remembered this from one of my father's conversations at dinner years ago.

I turned toward the other two-way mirror to see what was happening with Trevor. Moving closer to the window, I pressed the green button on the wall to eavesdrop on their conversation.

"So, Trevor. Can you tell me where you were on the night of September 4th?" Officer Wallace asked. "I was there starting around ten-thirty that evening."

Trevor's leg bounced up and down under the metal table like a pogo stick. Was he going to answer him? I knew where he was that night because I was there too, listening and watching.

"We can sit here all day, Trevor, or you can tell me where you were that night and then go home. It's up to you."

Trevor reached for the glass in front of him, but it was empty. The pitcher of water was out of reach. He licked his lips and swallowed. Did they want him to feel under pressure? Technically, he was, and the only way out was to talk. But if he said anything, then *they* would all be in trouble. He couldn't say a word. He couldn't let his friends get in trouble, too.

"Here, let me refill that glass for you," Officer Wallace said, lifting the half-full pitcher next to him. The ice cubes clinked against the pitcher as he poured some water into the cup.

My bladder stirred. *Great!* This *is not the moment to use the restroom.*

"You alright, man?" asked the officer leaning against the wall behind Trevor.

He looked familiar, but I couldn't recall his name, though he was the one who had driven me back to my mom's car after finding Paige's body. It wasn't important anyway. All I wanted was for Trevor to answer their questions so I could solve Paige's death and find out where Gavin was. Didn't he realize that the sooner he answered their questions, the sooner he could go home? They would let him leave, and it would all be over. I didn't know if that was true, but at least it would bring me closer to the truth.

Was it really that simple? If he told them where he was, he would also have to reveal who was with him. That would surely get *them all* into a heap of trouble. He must have felt trapped. Was there a way to avoid incriminating the others? I didn't know.

"I have to use the restroom," Trevor muttered.

"Answer our questions, and we'll let you go," replied the officer leaning against the wall.

A hint of laughter echoed behind the officer's words. Did he find this funny? Were they trying to make him pee his pants? Was this what my dad did to people when he interrogated them?

Trevor turned his head and stared at the officer behind him. A neatly trimmed beard covered the officer's face, making his eyes appear small. With his arms folded against his chest, he leaned back against the wall. His legs were outstretched and crossed at the ankles as if he were propping up the wall. His uniform was pressed neatly, with sharp creases running down each leg. I wondered if the officer reminded Trevor of his father. The man did resemble his dad quite a bit, especially with the beard.

The officer glared back at Trevor, neither of them looking away until a knock echoed in the room. The officer pushed himself off the wall and walked over to the door.

"Yeah, what do you need?" the officer grumbled.

"I have the kid's mother out here. She's upset and wants to see him," the woman said.

The bearded officer grunted. "Alright, let her in."

Trevor's face turned pale. He didn't want her there. I was sure he wouldn't speak once his mom entered the room.

"Hey, I still need to go to the restroom," Trevor said again.

"Rifkin, take him to the restroom and stay with him. Keep an eye on him," Officer Wallace said.

The officer's name was Rifkin, I repeated in my head.

Rifkin seized Trevor's arm and guided him out of the room and down the hall. Why were they treating him like this?

Thirty-Seven

Once Trevor left the room, I turned around to see what was happening with Mia. She hadn't moved, staying in the same chair since she arrived. Mia turned and glanced out the small window that overlooked the hallway. Her posture became tense.

Did she see Trevor walk by?

Mia's eyes widened as she slowly turned back toward the table, appearing paler now than when they had placed her in that room. I wanted so much to comfort her, but that would give me away; besides, I was eager to hear her confession. If Trevor wouldn't spill his guts, then that left Mia.

I couldn't take the chance of leaving this room and getting caught; besides, Mia would fold eventually. She was too fragile without Trevor beside her. She was probably scared out of her mind now that she had seen him.

I was a bit surprised that no one had come in since the officer escorted Mia to the room. They told her to sit and that someone would be in to talk to her. But that was, I twisted my wrist toward me and checked the time on my watch—almost an hour ago. It was now after five in the evening.

Looking back into the mirror, I watched as Mia smoothed her forefinger across the scar on her left wrist. It was a shade of pink and had a raised bubble appearance to it. Her eyes shifted to her other wrist, which had a similar matching scar but was an inch longer.

Each time Mia smoothed her finger over the scar, it sent a wave of nausea through my body. I shifted my eyes away. Not for fear of getting sick, but because I was sad for Mia. I wanted to know why. It had to be something horrible if she wanted to die and leave Trevor, the love of her life behind. And let's not forget her family. The way Mrs. B had acted last week clearly meant she wasn't over what Mia had done.

The door to Mia's room swooshed open, and a female officer stood in the doorway. "Can I get you anything while you wait for the Detective? Water or a snack?"

Mia shook her head. "No, I'm okay, thank you."

"Sure thing, sweetie. Just press this button on the wall if you need one of us." The female officer gestured toward a small white button located near the door.

"Okay," Mia nodded. "Thank you." The door closed. She continued to caress the scar on her right wrist until the sound of her cell phone ringing echoed through the room. I wondered if it was Trevor calling or texting her from the restroom. Alternatively, it could be her parents, curious about why she hadn't come home from school. My mind flashed back to earlier. Nope, there hadn't been any cars in the driveway, which meant they probably didn't know where their daughter was.

I imagined Mrs. B freaking out when she got home and found her beloved daughter missing from the house. There was no note to inform her that the police had taken her to the station. If Mrs. B was already acting frantic, this would surely push her over the edge.

Mia reached into her back pocket and pulled out her phone. She pressed the button on the side. Silence filled the air as she turned the screen toward herself. "Great, it's my mom," Mia muttered, taking a deep breath and sighing. She pressed the call button and held the phone to her ear.

"Hey, Mom. No, I'll be home a little later. I'm at a friend's house. No, it's not Kat. No, it's not Trevor. Just a friend from school. God, Mom, I'm fine, okay? Yeah, I'll be home before nine. Alright, yeah, bye." Mia ended the call and shoved her phone back into her pocket.

She lied to her mom. Why didn't she tell her the truth? Maybe she didn't want her to know that she was at the police station. Surely, her mom would think something terrible had happened. Yes, of course, she would. That's what mothers did best: they worried about everything concerning their children. Or perhaps she didn't want her mother to worry about her, considering what she did to herself. Mia's mom had been unstable the last time I saw her.

"Damn you, Gavin," Mia muttered. "Because of you, I'm here. I should have never gone into those woods with them. Then, I wouldn't be here for something I didn't do. I don't want to go to jail." Mia buried her face in her hands and cried.

I wanted nothing more than to hold her, but I couldn't. I had to stay strong and wait this out. My eyes fell to her wrist. She was wearing the friendship bracelet I had made and given to her in seventh grade. I pushed up the sleeve of my jacket to reveal the bracelet Mia had given me at the same time. God, I missed my best friend. How had we stayed apart for so long? When this was over, I would finally tell her how I felt—something I should have revealed months, or maybe even years, ago. I couldn't believe I had ended our friendship over a stupid boy.

Mia and I both jumped when the door to the interrogation room opened.

I swallowed.

It was the first time I would watch my dad in action. He stood by the door, closed it, and took a seat in front of Mia. He placed a small recorder on the table between them.

"Hey, Mia. It's been a while. How have you been?"

Both Mia and I furrowed our brows at the same time. Was my dad for real? Was he trying to be her friend? Was that how he got his information? Or was it because Mia and I used to be best friends, and she was always at our house? Did he see her like a daughter?

Mia wiped the tears from her face. "I'm not doing too well as you can see."

"Can I get you anything? Some Kleenex or a drink?"

"Yes, could I have some water, please?"

"Great! I'll be right back." He shuffled out the door and came back in under a minute. "Here you go." He held the glass of water in one hand and tissues in the other.

Mia took the tissues, wiped her cheeks, and blew her nose. My dad placed the cup of water on the table in front of her and then took a seat.

As he waited for her to finish drinking, he shuffled through some photos in the folder he had brought with him. I leaned forward, the tip of my nose touching the glass, but I still couldn't see the photos in his hand. He tilted them at an angle toward the table, waiting for Mia to finish drinking.

"I'll be recording the conversation while I ask you some questions." He pressed the red button on top. "I have a few photos to show you. If you can't bear to look at them for any reason, please let me know, and I'll turn them over." He flipped the first photo onto the table and pushed it toward her. "Do you know this person?" Detective Palmer asked.

Mia didn't make eye contact; she just nodded.

"Please respond with yes or no to the questions."

She nodded her head, then looked up at the detective. "I mean, yes. Yes, I know who that is."

"Can you state his name for the record?"

"Gavin Bowers."

"When was the last time you saw Gavin Bowers?"

"Um, I think it was Friday at school."

"You think it was Friday at school? Or are you sure it was Friday at school?"

Mia blinked and swallowed. "I'm more than sure it was Friday at school. Right before I left with Trevor."

"That's Trevor Chapman, right?"

"Is there another Trevor in this town?" Mia shot back.

He chuckled. "You make a good point. So, you saw Gavin at school on Friday before leaving with Trevor Chapman?"

"Yes."

"Did you see Trevor that night, around ten-thirty?"

The color drained from Mia's face. "No."

"Are you sure about that?"

She picked up the glass of water and took a mouthful, her cheeks puffing out like a bullfrog. After swallowing, she set the cup back down on the table. She coughed into her hand and then replied, "Yes, I'm sure. I wasn't with Trevor that night."

"I didn't ask whether you were with him. I asked if you saw him."

"Isn't that the same thing?"

"Yes, and no. Were you with Trevor on Friday, September 4th?"

"No."

He flipped another picture over and moved it closer to her. Mia's face turned pale as if she was about to be sick. "Can you tell me who you see in the picture?"

"It's me and Trevor," Mia whispered.

"And can you tell me the date and time in the top right corner of the photo?"

Mia swallowed. "September 4th at 10:35 p.m."

"The photo was taken at the light on Brewster and Fuller. The same night, you say you weren't with him. So, I'm going to ask you again. Were you with Trevor on the evening of Friday, September 4th?"

A single tear rolled down Mia's cheek. "Yes, I was with him."

"Where were you four headed that night?"

Mia's head shot up, her eyes wide. "The four of us?" she asked.

Detective Palmer set another photo on the table. “This is the same photo but enhanced. As you can see, there are two people in the back seat of Trevor’s car. Who were you with, and where were you going?”

Mia swallowed. “Jim and Paige.”

“Jim Covinski and Paige Ziel?”

“Yes.”

“So where were you headed to?”

“Lemmon’s Park.”

Detective Palmer nodded. “What were you four doing in Lemmon’s Park after dark?”

“We were there to talk to Gavin.”

“Gavin Bowers?”

“Yes.”

“What about?”

Mia looked up and fixed her gaze on the detective. “He sent this video to Trevor, Paige, and Jim.”

“What was in the video?”

Mia closed her eyes and then opened them again. “It was a video of the girl who was killed near Camp Wilson.

Thirty-Eight

My mouth dropped open as I stepped away from the glass. I had been right all along. Why did Jim deny it when I had seen the newspaper? I had read the article, yet Jim had lied to me. But why?

I glared at the two-way mirror, my face reddening with heat. He lied to me. He had swindled his way back into my heart and had deceived me to my face. Why? That was the only question repeating in my mind.

My father's voice snapped me back to reality.

"What was the video about? Do you have it?"

"Do I need a lawyer?" Mia asked.

"Did you kill the girl?"

"What! No, I didn't kill the girl. I was too busy trying to kill myself!" Her eyes widened in shock. She slapped a hand over her mouth and lowered her head.

Detective Palmer leaned forward and stopped the recording. "Mia, I'm sorry. Do you need a break?"

Mia didn't answer.

"Hey, I'm here if you ever need someone to talk to, alright? No recordings, no opinions. I'm just here to listen."

Mia lifted her head, her face streaked with tears and snot running from her nose. "I can't even talk to my own parents. What makes you think I can and would confide in you?" Her words came out sharp like a razor blade.

"Because sometimes it's easier to talk to someone outside the family. Someone who doesn't know you or your family very well."

"Then you wouldn't be a good person to talk to."

"Then I can find you someone else. Someone who can help you."

"What makes you think I need help? I already see a therapist twice a week."

"And?"

"And what?"

"Are they helping you?"

"Look." She leaned forward. "As much as you think you're helping me, you're not. I don't believe this..." Mia raised her elbows above the table, flipping her wrists over to reveal the scars. "Has anything to do with the case you're working on."

He nodded. "You're right, and once again, I'm sorry." Detective Palmer pressed the record button off and leaned back in the chair. "Let's continue then. Can you tell me what was on the video?"

Mia sighed. "It was dark and somewhat grainy, but it showed a girl lying on the ground."

"Was she alive?"

Mia shook her head. "No, I don't believe so."

"Continue."

"I didn't see any blood, but..." Mia paused. "I believe there was a knife sticking out of her chest."

His posture became rigid. With my father's back turned to me, I couldn't see his face.

"Knife?" he asked. He opened the folder in front of him and flipped through the papers until he found what he was searching for. Silence enveloped the room as he read.

I stepped closer to the mirror, waiting and listening.

"Detective Palmer, what's the matter?" Mia asked.

"Are you certain you saw a knife in the video?"

"Yes, I'm sure. I mean..." she paused, gazing off into space as if replaying the video in her mind. "The person recording the video zoomed in and out as if they were trying to capture the moment. But, as I mentioned, the video was grainy and, if you ask me, too dark to see what really happened."

"Do you have the video with you?"

"No." Mia relaxed against the chair.

"At home?"

She shook her head.

"Do you know who does?"

Mia chewed the inside of her cheek.

"I asked if you know who does?"

"As I said, Trevor, Jim, and Paige were all sent a copy."

Detective Palmer leaned over to stop the recording, then stood up. He opened the door to the room and walked out, closing the door behind him.

Thirty-Nine

I whipped around when the door swung open in the room where Trevor had been, but Trevor wasn't there anymore. My dad closed the door but didn't return to the room where Mia was. Did that mean he had gone searching for Trevor? I needed to get a hold of the video, but how? The only person left was Jim, and I was sure he wouldn't let me see it. He had denied that there was ever a dead girl, so showing me would only prove he had lied to me. I wondered what else he had been dishonest about. Did he truly love me, or was that a lie as well? He wanted to keep a close watch on me—to break into my phone and delete the pictures I had taken that night. My heart raced as heat rose to my face once again. I was glad that he wasn't standing in front of me at this very moment, or I'd rip his head off.

A loud shrill rang out from the hall. I cracked the door open to see who it was.

"Trev," his mom called as she hurried down the hallway. She ran to him and wrapped her arms around him.

"Mom," he whispered.

They let go of each other, but she kept him at arm's length, examining his face. "Are you alright? Did they do anything to you?"

Trevor narrowed his eyes; her question puzzled him.

Why would she ask that? They clearly hadn't done anything to him. He wasn't a criminal, though they were treating him like one.

"Are you charging him with anything?" his mom asked the officer standing behind Trevor. "Why is he here?"

"Mrs. Chapman let's go into a room, and I'd be happy to…" Officer Wallace began, but she interrupted him.

"A room? Why? What are you accusing my son of?"

"Ma'am, allow me to explain," Officer Wallace said.

"Explain to me while I'm standing here because we're not staying unless Trevor's under arrest. Has he been arrested?"

"No, we're not arresting him. We just have a few questions to ask him."

"Questions about what specifically?"

Officer Wallace let out an exasperated sigh. His shoulders tightened before sagging beneath his light-blue button-up shirt, the same uniform he had worn for the past ten years. "That's what I've been trying to explain. There's a classmate of his missing, and we were asking him if he knows where he is or if he has seen him," Officer Wallace explained.

"Who?" Mrs. Chapman asked.

"The boy's name is Gavin Bowers."

"Gavin Bowers?" Mrs. Chapman reiterated, gazing up at the ceiling before looking back at the officer and shaking her head. "I don't know any boy named Gavin. How about you?" She turned to her son. "Trevor, do you know a boy named Gavin? Do you go to school with him?"

Trevor stood upright, grabbing his throat and massaging it. His posture was twitchy. He glanced over his shoulder and down the hall in front of where they stood. Was he looking for an exit or for bystanders? Did he feel like they were ganging up on him?

My eyes scanned the hall. Other officers crowded around, staring at them, probably wondering what all the commotion was about. I stepped away from the door and peeked in on Mia. She was still sitting at the table, rubbing her scars, apparently unable to hear what they were discussing outside her door, which meant the rooms were soundproof. I moved toward the door.

"Answer the question," Officer Rifkin said from behind Officer Wallace.

"Ben," Mrs. Chapman murmured.

"Hey, Evelyn," Rifkin said, stroking his beard.

Trevor looked from the officer to his mom. "Um, Mom, can we go home now?"

Was he hoping that now his mom had shown up, he wouldn't have to answer any of their questions? Questions that could land him in serious trouble. But then again, this could be over if he just told the truth, if he was innocent, as he claimed. Why not tell them what happened? Because I sure would like to know.

"No," Officer Wallace replied. "We're going to sit down in there," he said, pointing his thumb toward the interrogation room where they had been seated. "You're going to answer our questions, and then you're free to go. You'll only look guilty if you don't answer."

Trevor's eyes shifted from his mom to Officer Wallace.

"Alright, let's get this done," Mrs. Chapman said, taking hold of Trevor's arm and leading him toward the room.

Officer Wallace led them across the hall and into the room next to mine.

"Do you or don't you know Gavin Bowers?" Officer Wallace asked again as the three of them took a seat. Officer Rifkin leaned against the wall as he had earlier.

"Yeah," Trevor said, slumping back in the chair. "We go to school together, but we're not friends. He's in different classes than I am."

"Alright, you claim you're not friends, but let's take a look," Officer Wallace said while rifling through some papers. "It states here that everyone witnessed Gavin getting out of your car on the first day of school."

Trevor stared ahead; his eyes wide open.

Was he really that stupid? The entire school saw him with Gavin.

"Do you mind telling me why, if you're saying you're not friends, he was in your car that morning? And here it says— and I quote, 'I want you to be nice to Gavin and get to know him. He'll be hanging around with us from now on.' This was what you told some of your teammates," Officer Wallace concluded.

"If you know this, then why are you scrutinizing my son?" Mrs. Chapman asked.

"Gavin has been missing since last Friday, and your son was the last person to see or talk to him. We want to find out if he knows where Gavin might be or where he could have gone. His mother is worried about him."

"Trevor, is that true?" Mrs. Chapman asked.

After a lengthy silence, Trevor nodded.

"Then tell them what you know."

"I can't because I don't know where he is, Mom," Trevor protested. "Yeah, I drove him to school, but only on the first day. And, yeah, I told my teammates to be nice to him, but then I decided to forget *him.* Why do I have to be nice to a kid who deserves to be bullied?"

"Trevor Joseph Chapman, don't you ever say that someone deserves to be bullied! I raised you better than that. Your father would have punished you for talking like that."

"Then it's a good thing he's not here," Trevor replied. His expression went blank. It was too late to take the words back.

His mom gasped.

I was surprised that his mom hadn't slapped him across the face for what he said. Instead, she cried, covering her face with her hands.

Trevor placed a hand on her back and pulled her close. "Mom, I'm sorry. I didn't mean to say that. It's just that..." he hesitated. "Gavin's not as nice as everyone thinks he is." He whispered something into his mom's ear, and she pulled back, staring at him.

"Oh, my God!" she gasped again.

Trevor nodded.

I stepped closer to the mirror, hoping to hear the whisper through the wall. The door behind me opened.

Forty

"What in the flying hell are you doing in here?" yelled Officer Grady. Her small, round, beady eyes shifted from me to the two-way mirror in front of me. "You can't be in here, especially during an interrogation." The officer reached out and grabbed my left elbow, pulling me toward the open door. "Come on, let's go before your father catches you in here, Kat."

"I want to hear what he has to say. I need to know what happened to Gavin," I pleaded, stumbling toward the door.

"I'm sorry, but I can't allow that. When are you gonna' mind your own business, darling? I should've known you weren't here to see your father. You hardly come to the station since your momma passed away."

We stepped out into the hall, and Officer Grady closed and locked the door behind us. "Heavens to Betsy, girl! What were you thinking? I reckon you have a suitable answer for this? Ya' always do."

I nodded.

Officer Grady raised her finger and glanced over her shoulder. “Come on, let’s find a place where we can talk in private.”

I followed the officer down the hall and into a room no bigger than my parents' bedroom at home. The thirteen-by-thirteen storage room held five shelving units: one along each wall and two in the center. They were all stacked with boxes labeled “office supplies.”

“Spill it,” Officer Grady said as soon as the door closed, leaving us alone.

I told her everything, surprised that the woman’s head didn’t fall off from how much she kept nodding at my every word.

“I wish I could help you, darling, but my hands are tied. You’re fixin’ to get into trouble; that’s what you’re doing. Leave it to the police. Your daddy will solve this case; you can bet your neighbor’s cat on that. Go on home now, and let us do our job. Ya’ hear me?” Officer Grady walked around me as if I hadn’t said a word and opened the door; her back turned to me.

I stood with an unfocused gaze at the officer like a deer caught in the headlights. Was this a dream? Was I home, in bed, dreaming all this up? No, but I had just jeopardized everything by telling Officer Grady what I knew, yet she didn't care. She was throwing me out to the curb like a piece of trash.

"Wait!" I shouted. "What are you going to do? Gavin is the key. If we find him, we can solve the case. Trevor knows what happened. Please, I'm begging you. And Mia, too—she knows something. They both do."

Officer Grady turned around in the doorway. She took a step forward and closed the door behind her. "Darling, you almost got yourself arrested last year when you broke into Harold's garage, looking for stolen goods, which the police found in a locked room there. You got lucky, girl, but this sounds more dangerous than just some stolen goods. You need to be careful. I know you know better, yet you seem to find yourself in a heap of trouble from time to time," Officer Grady said, shaking her head. She wiggled her pointer finger in the air. "Here's what I reckon I'm gonna do. I'm gonna go back to my desk and do my job. You, little lady, are gonna go home. I don't want to hear another word. Leave the case to us. We'll find Gavin and get the answers we need. Don't you worry, your pretty little head? Are we clear?" she said, resting her hands on her hips.

Part of her reminded me of my mother. She was a *take-charge* kind of woman. I nodded, but I couldn't leave well enough alone. I was determined to do something foolish, like drive back out to Lemmon's Park. I was sure that was where

I'd find the answers. Or some clue that would lead me to Gavin.

Forty-One

Beams of light filtered through the trees as I drove past the parking lot and onto the access road—the same road Trevor had taken that night with Gavin. I still wondered where his car had disappeared. Had someone taken it, or had Gavin left it? If he left, where had he gone if he hadn't gone home? This was what I needed to uncover, though I wasn't sure if the answers would be here. Something was drawing me back to this park. Something was waiting to be discovered.

Leaves lifted from the ground and twirled in the air like a small tornado, then gently floated back down. Twigs snapped under the tires of my car as I drove toward the cliff where we had all been that night.

I shut off the ignition and stared out the windshield. The sun had dropped behind the hills of the valley, leaving behind a purple night sky edged with pink and orange. I had an hour or so before dark. I climbed out of the car and walked to the open area. This time, I closed my eyes and envisioned the scene once again. I recalled a scream like someone was falling and then running right before Trevor's car sped away from the scene.

I opened my eyes and walked to the edge of the cliff. Though I had done this before, something compelled me to look over the bluff again. If they had chased Gavin as I remembered, he would have fallen over the side where I was standing now. Peering over the edge, I noticed for the first time a small area to the left where a person could have landed. If they had fallen to the right, they would have gone beyond the flat section of the cliff. No way could a person survive a fall like that, which ended on jagged rocks.

How did I not see that before? So, it was possible Gavin had fallen onto that flat area and later climbed back up and left. According to Officer Wallace, Gavin hadn't gone home. His mother was searching for him. I still wondered if he was the one who hit me. It was possible. Gavin could've climbed back up the hill, spotted me holding his phone, and knocked me out. He then hightailed it out of there, leaving me for dead and making the anonymous call to the police.

My mind grasped the idea that this was what had happened. Would he have made the anonymous call? I shook my head, doubting that was true. Gavin wouldn't care whether I lived or died. Not after how I had treated him last week. At least the Gavin I had known all these years only cared about himself. Look what he had done to the only best friend he ever had.

I scanned the scenery below. It would have been hard for Gavin to climb the hillside in the dark. He wouldn't have been able to see where to grab, which could have caused him to fall to his death. There had to be a path leading away from the flat area, assuming he had landed in that spot.

I moved to the right, searching for a way down, but found nothing. Racing back the other way, careful not to get too close to the edge, I spotted a narrow trail leading down the hill. My head tilted toward the sky. The sun was setting. I had to hurry.

Every few minutes, I glanced behind me and up at the cliff, then down at the ground. "If someone were to have fallen, they would be in that area," I murmured. The small tree I had held onto to look over the cliff was still visible. I would have to leave the trail to reach the area where I believed Gavin might have fallen. *If he fell at all*. This was true as well, but I still needed to search the area to be sure. I hadn't seen him fall. My mind retraced all the events of that night.

Was there a delay? The running, the car doors slamming shut. Yes, there was a brief pause, which could give someone enough time to push the front seat forward and for two people to hustle into the backseat. Trevor could have started the car while they climbed into the back, recalling the doors slamming and then the roar of the engine. But there was no sound of a third door slamming shut, which I knew because Gavin's car was still there after they had left the scene.

Shaking the images away, I trudged forward through the tall grass that reached the middle of my calf. Seconds later, I stood in front of a flat area. "*Look for anything,"* I told myself. I pulled out my cell phone and turned on the flashlight, directing the light onto the ground. It wasn't anything on the ground that caught my attention, but rather the broken tree branch rooted in the earth. Someone or something had snapped that branch as *if they had fallen on it or grabbed it.*

I walked over and inspected the branch. It exhibited signs of wetness, not dried out like wood would be if it had been broken for a long time. This could mean only one thing: It had been cracked recently.

I stood in front of the sapling, a few feet above my head. Someone must have grabbed the branch to stop themselves from falling. Someone like Gavin, who was a foot taller than me and had long, slim arms. Someone with that build could have touched the ground with their feet. Though, they wouldn't have known they were on flat land—a parcel that jutted out just enough for someone to land on. But depending on the person's angle, they might have missed the area and continued to fall until... well, until they hit the bottom, which I had already assumed. So, it was luck that this small tree had grown here for someone to grab hold of and survive the fall.

My mind recapped as I remembered hearing someone call for help that night. So, I was right; Gavin had fallen in this spot, hurt to the point where he needed someone to assist him. If he didn't walk out of here, then someone must have carried him. Of course, he wouldn't have known there was a path leading to this area, nor that he could walk right out until daylight. This raised even more questions.

Let's say he fell here where I stood and couldn't find his way out. That night, there had been a dark overcast. Even I struggled to see what was happening. His cell phone was up on the hill, but I was unsure how it had ended up in the weeds. Had someone thrown it in there? In hindsight, Gavin would have had to wait until dawn. So, who hit me over the head? That was another thing I needed to figure out. But for now, I needed to search for clues.

I snapped a picture of the sapling and inspected the area around me. I scanned the scene for blood, but I recalled that it had rained twice in the past week, which would have washed away any traces of blood and possibly any other evidence.

There was nothing down here, but that still didn't mean no one had been here. Using the flashlight from my cell phone to guide me, I turned and headed back the way I had come. A sparkle caught my eye. There was something in the weeds. I moved closer; the object glinted back at me as I shone the flashlight on it. It was a watch. I took several pictures and then bent over to pick up the item. Studying the watch, I noticed it wasn't just any watch but an Oulm men's sports watch.

Forty-Two

I picked up the watch and examined it more closely. The band was broken on one side. I wasn't sure exactly what that meant or how it had ended up down here, but I knew who the watch belonged to. Sure, someone else could own the exact same watch, but what were the chances they had been here in the past week and at the same time? Slim, I was sure. The inscription on the back narrowed the chances of it belonging to anyone else. Now, I had to find out what *he* was doing down here. More importantly, what this person had done with Gavin.

My breath came in quick bursts as I hurried up the path. Darkness enveloped me, wrapping around me like a warm blanket on a cold winter's day. I hadn't bothered to shine the light on the ground as I sprinted up the hillside. I tripped twice on the rocks jutting from the earth, skinning my knee on the rough ground. My heart raced, and I scrambled to my feet, ignoring the sharp pain spreading up my leg. I didn't want to stop until I reached the top. Once there, I bent over, placing my hands on my thighs, gulping in the air. I closed my eyes and steadied my breath. A wave of dizziness clouded my mind. I thought I might pass out from panting too hard. Seconds later, my breathing stabilized. I stood and limped toward my car.

"I can't let you leave, Katherine," a voice called from behind me.

My body froze.

The *thump, thump, thump* of my heartbeat pounded in my ears.

I swallowed, bile scorching the back of my throat.

I felt a sinking feeling in my stomach.

This couldn't be happening, but it was, and there was nothing I could do about it. My breath quickened in and out, just like that night—the night of the awful scream that still haunted me. I was sure the scream had come from Gavin, but his body wasn't here. At least, not now. So where was he? It had been almost a week. From the broken watch in my hand, I guessed he didn't climb back up but was carried away. If he was rescued, then where was he now? Why had this person taken him? The questions kept replaying in my head over and over, as if repeating them would jog a memory loose.

The answers were clear, but I didn't want to believe they were true. If I accepted the truth, my world would come crashing down around me—more now than it had when my mother died or when I walked away from Jim. Jim, whom I loved with all my heart, was only protecting me from what I was about to uncover. I didn't want to turn around because if I did, it would make the realization all too real. And if it were true, then everything else was a lie. My entire life was one big, fat, effing lie!

"Katherine Ann, please stop."

There was only one person who called me by my first and middle name. I didn't expect him to be here, but I knew the watch belonged to him—a watch I had given him as a Father's Day gift two years ago. I had it inscribed: *'To the moon and back, Your Loving Daughter, Katherine Ann.'* He wore it every single day until I woke up in the hospital and asked him about the watch. What did he say? My mind rewound back to that day. He claimed it was stolen during that break-in, but I knew that wasn't true. I looked at the watch in my hand. How many lies had he been telling me? And how long had he been lying?

I turned around; he was now ten feet away from me. No leaves crunched or twigs snapped as he moved closer. Almost stealth-like. He was skilled at sneaking around. Had he been the one to trash our home? But that would mean he had hit himself on the head. What kind of person would do that? Well, I was about to find out. His mouth parted, but I spoke first.

"Dad," I whispered.

My throat tightened as I stepped back, flinching when my body brushed against the car frame. I trembled, not from the coolness around me but from fear—fear of what my father would do now that I had pieced everything together. Now that I knew it was him.

My father.

My protector.

The man I had idolized my entire life.

He was the only person I had left, the only person I would have never imagined doing something so…so unimaginable to another person. Had he always been like this? Before, during, or did he change after my mom passed away?

I couldn't believe that four months had transformed a person into someone capable of hurting another. Killing someone else, but I didn't know if he had actually done it. I had seen nothing. I was speculating based on the evidence. Besides, I was there the night Gavin disappeared, and my father wasn't with them or with us. Was he? It was Trevor who chased Gavin, not my father, so why was I thinking he had hurt someone?

My mind was a jumbled mess as I tried to piece the fragments together. His long nights at work, before and after my mom died—of course, I never questioned him. A detective's job is stressful, and sometimes they have long, unpredictable hours, but we lived in a small town where bad things don't always happen. I didn't want to believe my father was a murderer. *Murderer.* Why was I even thinking this? That he would intentionally hurt another person.

He moved closer. "Please, let me explain," my father urged.

"Explain?" My voice trembled. What was there to explain? Then it struck me. He was acknowledging the truth. Confessing. *No, no, no,* my mind screamed. Not my father.

"Katherine, it was an accident."

"What constituted an accident?"

The words from the article surfaced in my mind, along with what Mia had said about the girl in the video. I recalled the way my father reacted when Mia mentioned the knife. *If it were an accident, then why was there a knife involved?* my mind questioned. "The knife," I whispered, watching as his body tensed up.

"What?"

He didn't know I was in the interrogation room. He hadn't realized I was watching, listening to every word. "If it was an accident, then why did you stab her with a knife?"

"How did you know about the knife?"

I actually had it all wrong. I hadn't read the article about the girl who was stabbed multiple times. My father told me she had been stabbed. Was that why the newspaper was missing? So, I couldn't verify the truth? But what confused me was Jim. Did he know it was my father all along? Was that why he was around more, to protect me? Would my father kill me? I slapped a hand over my mouth, choking back a cry.

"I was protecting you," my father said.

My eyes darted from side-to-side. There was nowhere for me to go; besides, he was too close. I couldn't run without him catching me, especially with an injured leg.

"Please, don't make this any more complicated than it is."

"Complicated?" The word escaped my lips. "You think I'm the one making this complicated? I'm not the one going around killing people." It struck me at that moment: the images of her body on that bed. "No," I muttered. "Did you kill Paige too?"

Forty-Three

He was gazing at the ground when he suddenly looked up and stared at me, blinking repeatedly.

Every movement.

Every expression.

His failure to defend himself was all the answer I needed to know that he indeed killed Paige as well. "Why? Why did she have to die?"

He shook his head. "I don't know what you mean. I didn't hurt her. I did the same thing you did. I was out here looking for Gavin."

"What?" I glanced around as if searching for answers. Did he kill Paige or that girl?

I followed his gaze as he tilted his head back and squinted up at the sky. Stars twinkled as if they were blinking back at us. Time had somehow eluded us as night fell. The moon cast a soft white glow all around us. Bullfrogs croaked, and crickets chirped. Like that night, everything changed for me. I inhaled the scent of fresh evening air and shivered.

Everything returned to that night: the girl killed nearby, and then Gavin and Paige. After a long silence, he answered.

"You."

"Me?" I looked back down into my father's eyes, my mind going blank. What on earth was he talking about?

"Yes, you and Gavin…"

My eyes darted from side-to-side as I searched my memory of that night. Someone had struck me on the head and knocked me out. I glanced up at my father. "Wait!" I interrupted. "You were out here that night?" I shook my head. "But how? I had the car."

"I received a notification the moment you left the house. I've set it up on my phone to alert me when you go. Not that you ever go anywhere, but you were invested in this case. You wouldn't rest until you solved it. It was for your own protection, Katherine. I took your mother's car and followed you out here." He ran a hand through his hair, just like he always did. "I heard everything they said. I saw everything that happened out here. Then they fled the scene, and you emerged from the woods. I knew you were here somewhere; I just didn't know exactly where you were hiding. I didn't want to take my phone out to find you. Of course, you went searching for clues." He shook his head. "I don't know why you insist on getting involved when all it does is lead you into controversial, dangerous, and foolhardy situations?" he asked, sounding almost disgusted.

That explained why there was no dust on the tarp covering my mom's car. Then my mind flashed back to that night when I heard a branch snap, thinking it was a deer. After that, I found Gavin's phone again. Then everything went dark. "You? Are you the one who hit me over the head?"

"No!" he shouted. "I didn't see you. It must have happened after I carried him up the hill."

"Gavin?" I asked, imagining the scene unfolding before me. My father had come here and witnessed everything. He saved Gavin, but if he rescued him, then where is he? "Where is Gavin? What did you do with him?"

"I carried his body up the hill and..." he paused, glancing back up at the sky.

I wasn't sure, but were those tears running down his cheeks? "What did you do with his body?"

A heavy sigh escaped his throat. "I took care of everything. Can't that be enough?" my dad said. "Can't you leave well enough alone? I did it for you."

Me? My mind questioned. What did this have to do with me? Nothing made sense. He wasn't making any sense. In that split second, I jolted away from the car. Away from him. I wasn't sure where I was going or what I was doing; I just wanted to run. To get away from him. Gavin had to be out here somewhere; I was sure of it. *Where else could he be?*

"Katherine, wait!" he shouted. "If you're searching for Gavin, you won't find him here."

I came to an abrupt stop, barely hearing the words escaping his lips. I wouldn't find him because my father must have buried him somewhere out in the woods. Acres and acres of woods. I turned around and marched toward my father, halting just a foot away from him.

Crow's feet spread alongside each eye. *When had he started to get those?* So much had happened this year; I paid little attention to anyone else because of my own grief. But how had I missed everything going on around me? This man, who had taught me how to solve mysteries, was the reason I was out here following my classmates. They were hiding something, and now two of them were dead.

Jim.

I hadn't seen him for two days. I swallowed the bile rising in my throat. "Did you do something to Jim?"

"What? No! He's the only smart one in the group. He keeps to himself; besides, I did you a favor." He pointed a finger at my chest.

"You did me a favor? What did you do to him?"

He raised a hand to stop me. "I didn't hurt him, if that's what you're implying."

“Then what? What am I supposed to believe after everything I’ve heard tonight?” Sweat beaded on my forehead and trickled down my temple. Anger simmering inside me. Why was I suddenly so hot? I was nothing like him. Nothing like my father. I would never kill anyone.

“I told him to stay away for a while and that it was best for you two to take a break from each other, as he was upsetting you. I think he was trying to figure things out, Katherine. I couldn’t let him find out what happened to his friend and that girl.”

“Was Gavin still alive when you found him?”

“Yes.”

“So, why eliminate him?”

“The girl.”

My mind raced, searching for answers until it fell into place. “The girl who was killed. What did he have to do with her? You said you killed her.”

“I said it was an accident.”

“An accident is someone falling and getting hurt, not getting stabbed multiple times. And that doesn’t explain what Gavin had to do with any of it.” Part of me wanted to grab my father by the shoulders and shake him. Why was he playing this cat-and-mouse game with me? Just tell me the freaking truth! Stop beating around the bush.

“I did everything to protect you.”

Forty-Four

I turned and stumbled away. I didn't want to hear anymore. My father was a killer—a murderer.

He grabbed my arm and pulled me back toward him. I flinched at his touch, the same touch that had comforted me every time I felt sad. Now, I recoiled in fear—fear that he would hurt me now that I knew what he was and what he would do to me. This person I didn't even recognize anymore. Maybe I hadn't known my father at all my entire life. It was all one big effing lie.

I took a few steps away from him. The acidic taste in my mouth made my stomach churn. I needed water, which was in my car—the one behind him. I walked around him and opened the car door. As I reached in to grab the water bottle, my body was yanked back. My father had seized the belt loop of my pants and pulled me out of the car.

"What the hell, Dad!" I shouted, turning around and pounding my fists against his chest.

"I can't allow you to leave."

"I wasn't leaving; I was just getting some water." Twisting out of his grip, my head nearly hit the outer roof of the car. As I lost my balance, I fell onto the driver's seat, my back smacking against the steering wheel, causing me to wince in pain. I turned and bent forward; my feet firmly planted on the ground as I rubbed the right side of my lower back. The throbbing eased. Reaching behind me, I grabbed the bottle of water.

I held it up to show my dad, then unscrewed the lid, and guzzled the entire bottle. I threw the empty container over my right shoulder and onto the passenger side floor.

"Gavin was in the woods that night. He had filmed the girl. The only thing missing from the video was me. But… he took the knife with him. The knife that had fingerprints on it?"

"How can the video convict you if you're not even in it?"

My father looked away, then back down at me. "He saw me standing in the woods after Trevor, Paige, and Jim had fled the scene. He was still holding his phone. I'm pretty sure he was still recording. He ran off. I couldn't stop him. I was certain he was going to call the police, but he never did." He ran a hand down his face. "I left and went home, leaving her body there to be found. I showered and burned the clothes I had been wearing. I made sure there was no trace of that night anywhere. I went to work the next day, scared they knew something." He shook his head. "But when I got there, the Captain handed me a fresh case. I said nothing. It was as if it had never happened. Though I wish that were true, but…"

My mind went back to the first day of school almost two weeks ago. Gavin stepped out of Trevor's car and then tried to persuade Paige to date him. Earlier, Mia had mentioned a video being sent to all of them at the police station. I looked up at my dad. "I think Gavin was using the video to blackmail them into doing what he wanted, even though you were the one who killed her?"

My father flinched at my words, looking confused. "I don't know what you mean."

"Yes, you do. You said that Gavin recorded the girl and that he had been out there that night when the others left the camp and went into the woods. The same girl they were all standing around. This means Gavin was using it to blackmail them into gaining popularity or playing some sick game he had fabricated in his mind." I told my father what I had overheard on the first day of school. I placed my head in my hands, exhausted by the night's events and unsure of what I should do.

My father didn't hurt me, even though he said he couldn't let me leave here. I didn't know what to do or how to feel. My dad killed Gavin because he knew the truth about what my dad had done. What role did Paige play in all of this? "What happened to Paige?"

"What do you mean?" He shrugged. "You were at the cabin. You saw her lying there dead."

"Didn't you take her to the cabin and lay her down in that bed? Didn't you strangle her?" Nausea washed over me once more.

"No, I didn't. I already told you that I didn't kill her."

I was missing something. Had Paige come back out here that same night? If so, when? No, that would have been impossible unless she requested to get out of the car. There was no way she could have gone home and returned here in such a short time. I couldn't ask her because she was dead. But the others would know. They had been with her. She might have come back after my father left the scene. It had to be while I was wandering around in the woods. But then, I would have heard her car. Seen her car. That was if she had driven here, though I couldn't imagine her walking, especially at night, alone. Perhaps she was the one who broke the branch I heard snap. Had she been the one to report me? Maybe hit me over the head? More questions surfaced than answers.

"So, did you kill Gavin, or was he already dead from the fall?" I asked.

"No, he was still alive when I went down there. I carried him up the hill."

"Is that when you lost your watch?"

He nodded. "The band must have broken, but I didn't realize it until I got home that night. I searched everywhere for it, but..."

"But I found it first?"

"Yes."

I placed my head between my legs as it spun in circles like a merry-go-round, feeling faint. It was all too much. All I wanted was to drive away. To get far away from here. Away from him. Away from me. I should turn him in. But I still didn't know the whole truth. I needed to call the police, but how? There was no way he would let me use my phone to call anyone. Would he hurt me like he did the others to save himself? But I was his daughter; surely, he loved me and wouldn't harm me. Still, I couldn't let him leave here. I couldn't let him continue doing this.

I lifted my head. My father was looking down at the ground, which meant he didn't see the expression on my face.

Forty-Five

My eyes widened, and my lips parted slightly as I mouthed the word "Jim." I flinched when the thick wooden branch struck the back of my father's skull. He fell to the ground like a bird crashing into a glass window. I had no time to stop Jim.

"Oh, my God!" I shouted, leaping to my feet.

"Kat, are you alright?" Jim asked.

"Yes, I'm fine. How did you… Where did you come from?" I asked, glancing around and noticing that his car was nowhere in sight.

"I need to know that you're alright. That he didn't harm you."

"No, I'm okay. He didn't harm me."

"Good. Let's put him in the trunk of your car before he wakes up."

I nodded but didn't budge from my spot.

"Kat," he said, placing his hands on my arms and giving me a little shake as if to jolt me out of my zone. "You need to help me. Grab his arms."

I reached into the car and pressed the button under the dashboard. The trunk popped open. Then I took hold of my dad's arms while Jim grabbed his legs. We staggered to the back of the car. I didn't realize how heavy my dad was.

"Ready? Lift," Jim grunted.

Neither of us was strong, but we were able to lift my dad into the spacious trunk. We stood there, looking down at him.

"How much did you hear?"

"Enough to realize he isn't the person I believed he was."

"That makes two of us."

Jim lifted his arm and slammed the trunk lid down.

"Now what?" I asked, then I wondered how Jim got here. "How did you get back here? I didn't hear your car!"

"I parked at Camp Wilson and walked through the woods. I heard both of you talking and what he had said."

"What were you doing at camp?"

Jim looked down, then up into my eyes. "I was saying goodbye to Paige. That's where she died, I assume. I feel guilty because she would still be alive if it weren't for finding..."

"Finding that girl dead in the woods," I said. "The same girl you claimed didn't exist."

"I figured that since you couldn't remember anything, I'd share a different story that would be forgotten."

"Except, I remembered everything."

“If we hadn’t come out here that night to face Gavin, you wouldn’t have gotten hurt, and Paige...”

“And Paige would still be alive.” I understood what he was saying, but I wasn’t sure where we would go from here. So much had happened, and all I wanted to do was rewind time and go back to the first day of school. Climb off the bus and walk straight into the building without looking back. Mind my own business as I should have, but that wouldn’t change what I had discovered: that my father was a murderer. Did that mean my dad would still be hurting and killing people if I had done things differently? Or would they have caught him? I didn’t know the answer to those questions.

“I’ll go with you to the police station,” Jim said.

"Is that it? We’re really just going to turn him in?” I looked at Jim with a blank expression.

He cupped my face with both hands and looked deeply into my eyes. “I... I just don’t know, Kat. You heard what he said. He killed that girl and then disposed of Gavin’s body.”

“Yeah, but you and Trevor made Gavin fall over the cliff,” I shot back, tears streaming down my face. “You don’t see me rushing to the police to tell them what happened, do you?”

Jim stepped back as if I’d punched him in the gut. “I never meant for this to happen. We were just supposed to talk to him and get him to stop threatening us, but he kept pushing and pushing, and then Trevor chased him. It was so dark outside. It was an accident, Kat. An accident." Sobs echoed around me as he cried.

For the first time since I had known Jim, I had never seen him cry. It was rare for boys or men to show this kind of emotion, especially in front of girls. Did that mean he felt guilty for what happened that night? Of course, he did.

"Why did you all leave? Why didn't you try to help him?"

"How? It was so dark outside. We assumed he had gone all the way down," Jim replied. "And Trevor—Trevor started running toward his car, and I followed. We all followed him."

My head bobbed up and down as my mind flicked back to that night. Yes, it had been dark, and yes, I, too, had peered over the edge and saw nothing. I didn't know until today that there was a ledge where he had landed. "Yes," I said in agreement. "But you could've called for help. The firefighters would have searched for him, and none of this would be happening right now. Gavin would be here."

"And your dad would be in jail."

I shook my head.

"Kat, we can't let him go. He'll kill again. There's something seriously wrong with your dad. You have to see that." Jim stepped closer to me, placing a hand on my left arm and gently moving it up and down in a soothing manner.

Another tear slid down my face, falling from my chin to the ground. He was right about my dad, but he was all I had left. Where would I go? Where would I live? I wouldn't be eighteen for another two months. Jim pulled me into a hug as I cried.

We were forehead to forehead, gazing into each other's eyes until the sound of branches cracking interrupted us, signaling a vehicle driving up the road toward us. We sprang apart, exchanging looks before turning our attention back to the road ahead.

"Shit, shit, shit," Jim cursed. "Who the hell is that?"

"I'm not sure, but what if my dad wakes up? How are we going to explain why he's in the trunk?"

"Okay, here's what we'll do. You'll get in the car and drive away from here. I'll meet you at the old barn on Creek Road. Park behind the barn and stay put." He kissed me on the lips. "Everything will be fine. I promise."

I got into the driver's seat and drove down another dirt road, away from the vehicle that had just arrived at the clearing where Jim was still standing.

A 1998 San Marino Red Honda Prelude.

Forty-Six

Why would Trevor be coming to Lemmon's Park? Was he there to see Jim? A part of me wanted to stay and figure out what they were up to. Were they planning something? No, because Jim said he had walked from the cabins. I'll have to ask him once he meets me at the barn.

My fingers went numb from gripping the steering wheel, so I released one hand and shook it. Blood returned to my fingertips, transforming my pale skin into a deep shade of pink. Then, I repeated the process with my other hand.

Blinking back tears, I drove down the familiar path. I spotted my dad's car parked along the side and drove around it. I recalled this same path from the day I discovered Paige in the cabin. I hadn't realized there was another access road into Lemmon's Park until that day, which indicated it was quite new since I hadn't been out here since my mom passed away. If I had, I would have taken it the night we all came out here.

Once I reached the main road, I drove for miles until the barn appeared in sight. I turned left, parked behind the barn, and turned off the engine. I rested my head against the steering wheel. What was I going to do now? My dad killed a girl and then tried to cover it up. Not just that girl, but Gavin and Paige too. Though he claimed he had nothing to do with Paige's death, I wasn't sure I believed him. How many others have there been? How long has he been at this?

I feared what the police might do or, worse, what the prisoners would do. The criminals he had arrested could kill him if he ended up in the same prison as them. But wasn't he a monster himself? Didn't he deserve to be locked up with the rest of the murderers?

Thinking back on all the years I spent with my dad, I couldn't envision him as a killer. He had always been so kind and caring—someone who would have your back if you needed him. Sure, he sometimes came home late, but I had never once seen him with blood on his clothes. Something wasn't right.

Tingles crawled beneath my skin like spiders hatching from their eggs. Then it hit me. Although my dad had confessed, he hadn't made eye contact with me, which he only did when he was hiding something. But why would he lie? Was he covering for someone? If so, who?

I closed my eyes and let myself go back. Back when my mom was still alive. Back when I started dating Jim. Back to the start of summer. Before my dad sent me to Florida to visit my grandparents, he told me I needed time away, that my mother's death had taken a toll on me, and that I needed to heal from my breakup with Jim. But there was something else, something that had happened; I just couldn't remember what. It felt as if my mind had blocked it out.

A loud knock pulled me back to reality. It was coming from the trunk. My dad was awake. Would he try to escape if I opened it? Where the hell was Jim? Was he still with Trevor? I had to wait for him to show up. We hadn't bound my dad's hands or feet. He could overpower me. He would escape.

The knocking sounded again, and then he spoke.

"Katherine, please let me out of here. I'll explain everything to you," he pleaded. "I'll tell you the truth this time, I swear. Please, just let me out of the trunk."

Hadn't he explained everything earlier in the woods? Or was he going to hurt me like he did the others, then dispose of my body? I could hear what he had to say through the closed trunk. I wouldn't open it, just listen. Didn't I owe him that much? Well, I didn't owe him anything. He was a killer. A murderer who should be behind bars. Despite that, something felt off about what he'd said earlier. Call it a gut feeling if you must. I didn't believe he had killed or hurt anyone. So, if not him, then who?

I opened the car door and stepped out. A bitter, cool breeze hit me in the face. I shivered and wrapped my arms around myself to stay warm, but it didn't help. Why hadn't I come better prepared? Well, I hadn't known I was going to drive out to Lemmon's Park again to search for clues. I hadn't thought to bring extra clothing in case the weather changed. I hadn't realized I'd be locking my father in the trunk like a prisoner. I hadn't considered anything else; I just reacted. None of this should have happened. But if I were to be honest with myself, it's not like I sat down and plotted the entire event out like an agenda. I had to fix this.

As I closed the driver's side door, I noticed something on the backseat. I opened the rear door and found my mom's favorite gray cotton sweater—the one she always wore during our picnics. I grabbed it, quickly slipped my arms through the openings, and wrapped it around my chest, hugging the soft material close to me. It felt like she was with me, holding me in her arms. I pressed my nose into the fabric and inhaled deeply. My heart fluttered. I closed my eyes, allowing myself to see her and feel her presence. The fragrance of her perfume lingered in the fibers. My body filled with warmth.

A loud pounding vibrated through the car, startling me. My dad was still in the trunk. I walked toward the back of the car, staring down at the lid. All I needed to do was talk to him. No harm done. No opening of the trunk. No giving in to him or being persuaded. I hoped I was as strong as my mind believed I was. I needed to stand up to my father—something I had never done before. I hadn't ever had to. He wasn't a mean person. He held me when I cried and gave me advice when I needed it.

"Will you be honest with me this time? No lies." I listened for his response. When I didn't hear anything, a wave of dread washed over me. No, I wouldn't let him die. I needed to open the truck and let him breathe. He wouldn't hurt me, right? If he were going to kill me, he would have done it already.

I rushed to the driver's side door and yanked it open. I hit the trunk release and dashed back to the rear of the car, peering into the trunk. My dad lay unresponsive.

"Oh, God. Dad, what did I do?" I murmured. My heart raced in my chest. What would I do if he were dead? How would I explain it to the police? I needed to act. I reached down and placed two fingers on the side of his neck. There was a pulse. My muscles relaxed, but my heart was still pounding. I nudged his shoulders, and his eyes fluttered open.

"Dad," I murmured.

He took small, shallow breaths and then sat up.

"Stay!" I yelled, flinching at the sound of my own voice. I didn't understand why I shouted. He wasn't moving quickly enough to get away.

He rested his head in his hands. "I did it for you," he whispered.

I wasn't sure if I had heard him correctly. What did he mean by saying, '*he did it for me*'? "I don't understand. What did you do for me?" Something within me unraveled like an electric wire thrashing out of control. I felt drained by the lies my father and Jim were feeding me. All I wanted was the truth. "Tell me the truth!" I shouted through gritted teeth. Where was my anger coming from? Frustrated, I wanted to hit something. Heat filled my body, and my blood boiled.

"Katherine, stop," my father said as he reached for my arm.

I leaped away from his grasp. Suddenly, my body jerked. Crickets chirped all around me as I stood in the darkness. My head snapped to attention before I looked down at the ground. I was standing over a girl.

A girl with a knife in her chest.

Forty-Seven

"Wake up, Katherine."

My body shook as I gasped for air. I opened my eyes to see my dad kneeling beside me on the ground. Stars twinkled in the night sky above.

"Katherine Ann. Oh my God." He sounded as if he were crying, but I didn't see any tears on his face.

"What… what happened?" I choked out the words. My body swam in wooziness, similar to the effects of the pain pills the doctor had given me, even though I hadn't taken any. My breathing grew shallow. Was that why I was on the ground? Had I fainted?

"You blacked out again."

My eyebrows crinkled at his words. What did he mean *again?* Had I always blacked out? When and how often? His words confused me. I didn't remember ever experiencing this before, but maybe a person who had episodes of blackouts wouldn't remember. That was why they called them blackouts.

"Here, let me help you up." He put an arm behind my back and raised me into a sitting position.

"What the hell did you do to her?" a voice shouted from behind us.

We both turned and looked over our shoulders, not realizing that Jim had arrived. He came rushing toward us, his face red.

"I was helping her," my dad said.

"Get your hands off her," Jim shouted again. "Kat, why did you open the trunk? You had one job, which was to wait for me. You know he's dangerous."

"I... I thought he was dead. I got scared, so I opened the trunk to check on him," I stammered. Why did my father let Jim speak to him like that? He was a man of authority. Better yet, why was I letting him talk to me this way?

Jim hurried over to me, nudging my dad aside, and helped me stand up. I leaned against the car's bumper.

"Are you alright? Did he hurt you?" Jim asked as he looked for any signs of abuse.

"No," I shook my head. "He didn't do anything. I…" My mind spun, searching for clues as to what my dad had said before Jim showed up and practically ruined everything. I turned my head to look up at my father, who was frowning. Then, just as quickly as it had vanished, the image reappeared. I remembered that before my body plummeted to the ground, I had been standing above a girl with a knife in her. But the real question was why and whether it was real or just a figment of my imagination. "Dad?" I asked.

"Katherine, I was... I was hoping you wouldn't remember," my father said.

"What do you mean? Remember what?" I asked.

He cleared his throat. "You've been having incidents where you leave the house at night. I guess doctors would call it sleepwalking, except you seem awake. It's so hard to explain. Anyway, I follow you when that happens. The moment your bedroom door opens, I get an alert on my phone. I installed sensors on all the doors and windows in our house."

I stared at him, uncertain about what he was rambling on about. Sleepwalking? Alerts? Door sensors? What the hell was he talking about? "What are you talking about?"

"It began right after your mom was diagnosed, and then it got worse. I started to see things. So, I would stay up late and sometimes sleep on the sofa in the living room."

I shook my head. Of all the times he had slept on the couch, it wasn't because he was working on a case. "And what exactly am I supposed to do when I'm supposedly sleepwalking?" I asked, making air quotes with my hands.

He looked down at the ground, then at Jim, and back at me. "Well, at first, you wandered around the house, and sometimes you'd be in the backyard. Occasionally, I would find you sleeping in your mom's car." He rubbed the back of his neck. "After she passed away, things got much worse. I found you at the cemetery in the middle of the night, lying on her grave. That's why I had to send you to your grandparents over the summer: to give you a change of scenery and relieve the anxiety you were feeling over your mother's illness and her death."

He shifted his gaze toward Jim. "And your breakup with Jim. My parents said you were doing well. That you hadn't left the house at night while you were there. They even had an extra lock put on the door and kept the key with them at night, but said you never left your room," he smiled. "I was grateful that you were feeling better and knew it had to be this house. This neighborhood where you've lived since you were born. I wanted you to stay longer, but school was about to start, and you were begging to come home. So, three weeks before school started, I flew you back."

My dad ran his hand through his hair and began again. "You weren't home for a week when I followed you to Lemmon's Park. I can't believe you drove while sleepwalking, but I've read that it can happen. Your body can be in such a deep sleep that you do things without recalling them. You said you had trouble sleeping, so I gave you some pills to help you. Several hours later, you were leaving in your mom's car," he concluded. "I had hoped that being away would help you, but I was wrong."

"I don't understand," Jim said. "What does this have to do with you killing that girl and Gavin and Paige?"

My dad gave him a look. Jim flinched, stepping back.

"I think I remember that night. It was dark, and I had a blanket in the backseat along with Mom's favorite picnic basket. I was going to spread the blanket out and have lunch with Mom in the woods, where we would enjoy our meal," I said. "But then I heard something and..." I paused, searching deeper into my mind for the memory. I shook my head, unsure of the details. "I can't recall. I'm not sure what happened next."

"You must have been following the sound. When I arrived, you were standing over her, and there was a knife in her chest."

Forty-Eight

"Oh my God," Jim muttered. "*You* killed her? I think I'm going to be sick." With his hand covering his mouth, he stumbled away from us, running toward a tree. His retching made my stomach churn.

"I helped you walk away from her body. No one knew you were there. I laid you down on the ground, and you fell asleep. Nothing I did could wake you. I had never seen anything like it. My plan was to get you home, but before I could do that, I needed to grab the knife because it had your prints on it. Then, I heard voices, so I stayed hidden in the shadows. That's when Gavin noticed me and started filming. After Trevor, Paige, and Jim fled the scene, Gavin took the knife before I could reach it," Dad explained. "So, when your friends showed up at Lemmon's Park that night a week ago, I came too and followed. I didn't knock you out, I swear. When I came back up the hillside with Gavin over my shoulder, you weren't there. It was my only chance to make things right."

“So, if you didn’t knock me out, then who did?”

“I don’t know. I swear on your mother’s grave.” He raised a hand and then placed it over his heart.

“So, you’re not a killer; I am?”

“But you didn’t mean it. You were sleepwalking. Don’t you see? You didn’t have control over your thoughts or movements. It was like you were hypnotized.”

“I killed a girl,” I repeated, closing my eyes. I used what my dad said to piece together what might have happened that night. Small fragments surfaced as if I were seeing it through someone else’s eyes. I opened my eyes and stared at my dad, tears streaming down his face. I repeated everything I remembered out loud to him.

“Wait?” my dad asked. “The knife wasn’t yours?”

I shook my head. “No, at least I don’t think so.”

“Do you think someone else was there? Did you see anyone? Whoever was with that girl could have killed her. But then you showed up and…” my dad fell silent.

“And what?” I leaned in, waiting for his response.

“They saw you and ran away. Then I arrived, and I thought you had killed her.”

My eyes shifted away, allowing his words to sink in. “I don’t know. I can’t be sure.” I shook my head. How could I remember the events if I didn’t even know I was there? I relied solely on what my dad was saying—how he described the scene when he arrived, finding me there standing over her body.

“I believe it could be possible,” he said. “I don’t know why I didn’t consider it before. I don’t remember your clothes having any blood splatter on them.”

I nodded, yet I wasn’t sure what I was agreeing to. It all felt so unbelievable. *Sleepwalking?*

“If there was another person in the woods that night, which, the more I think about it, seems increasingly likely, they could have been the one who killed Paige too.”

“I’m not sure I understand.” My eyes moved from my dad to Jim, who had come back to my side, looking pale.

“At the cabin, the coroner mentioned that Paige had finger marks on her neck,” my dad said.

"It was as if someone had choked her," I concluded.

My dad agreed. “This means it’s possible that the same person who killed that girl also killed Paige. Unfortunately, we don’t know who they are or where they are now. They could be long gone.”

“Yeah, but if you remember, they said Paige had been dead for a couple of days. If that’s true, then who kept the fire going?” I asked.

My dad snapped his fingers. “You’re right. We also checked for fingerprints, so I’ll need to follow up on that when I get back to the station.”

"Wait!" Jim shouted. "So, if you didn't kill that girl, does that mean Kat is the one who killed her?"

We both turned and looked at Jim.

"No, there's no way she could have done it, but I can't be one hundred percent sure. I'm going to head back to the station and review all the evidence we collected at the cabin."

"What happened to Gavin's body?" Jim asked.

"I took him to a hospital outside of town, dropped him off, and left him leaning against the wall outside the entrance. I parked his car in the hospital parking lot and waited until a couple of hospital workers came outside and took him inside." He ran a hand through his hair. "I had worn gloves, so I didn't have to wipe away my prints, and then hiked back out to the woods. When I got back to my car at Camp Wilson, daylight had approached. I didn't know where you had gone, Katherine. My key problem was Gavin, and I obviously didn't have time to retrieve both vehicles when the call came through the police scanner that someone had found a body in Lemmon's Park.

"A hiker called it in, but they didn't leave their name." He rubbed a hand over his forehead, then, using his thumb and forefinger, rubbed his eyelids, pressing them toward his nose. "I got into my car and drove over there, and that's when

I saw you lying on the ground. It happened after I left with Gavin's body."

"Wait, Gavin isn't dead?" Jim asked.

Was he paying attention to anything my father said?

"No, he's fine, but the doctor says he has amnesia and doesn't remember what happened to him or the events from the past few months. Hopefully, he won't recall them. He didn't see you that night, Katherine; he saw me. If… if he puts the pieces back together, then it's me they will question, not you."

"So, why question Trevor and Mia if you knew where Gavin had been all along?" I asked. If my dad hadn't realized I was at the police station, he certainly did now.

His eyes narrowed and then softened. He understood what I was saying. "I had to pretend I didn't. Besides, I needed to know what they knew. Then Mia mentioned the video being sent to Trevor, Paige, and you," my dad said, looking at Jim. "I had to get that video before it ended up in the wrong hands."

"So, what brought you out here?" I asked.

"Officer Grady mentioned you were at the station. I checked my phone, and it showed you were on your way to Lemmon's Park again. So, I rushed out here, and that's when you came running up the hill. I knew you had found something; you were shaking uncontrollably."

I nodded and leaned against the car. Dizziness washed over me, and I didn't want to risk falling. I wished I could recall more about that night.

"So, what are we going to do?" Jim asked, moving closer and wrapping an arm around me to keep me steady. "I can't let anything happen to Kat, and I won't tell anyone. Besides, she doesn't know anything. And you said you didn't see her stab the girl, just standing over her. That could mean she didn't do it."

"Yes, she was sleepwalking," my dad replied. "I did some research on sleepwalkers and crimes they might commit. The officials will need to run tests on her to use in court if the evidence shows she committed the killing. According to several cases I found, the person must receive treatment for their mental health issues."

"And?" Jim questioned.

"And the court never convicted the sleepwalker of the crime because they were in a state of insane automatism, meaning they were acting involuntarily."

"So, she would just continue her life as if nothing happened?" Jim asked.

"Well, yes and no. If the evidence indicates that she was the one who killed the girl, she would likely be committed to a psychiatric hospital. But I'm not the courts, Jim. I can't be certain they won't convict her of the crime. Every case is different and decided by a jury, not by mental health doctors."

"Then we should get her help, right?" Jim asked. "Has she been sleepwalking since that night?"

"Dad," I said. "I don't want to end up in jail."

"You won't go to jail. Gavin doesn't remember, and I'll make sure it stays that way. And if… if he does start to remember, he didn't see you?" Dad stared at us. "Besides, we still don't have the murder weapon. Gavin took it and did something with it. As for your question, yes, I caught her sleepwalking in the past couple of weeks."

My head swam with confusion as I tried to recall the past week. Then, a flicker of recollection hit me: the dirt in my bed. Oh, my God, my dad was right. It all made perfect sense to me now.

"What happens next?" Jim inquired.

"We act as if this conversation never happened. We don't talk to anyone about it. Are we clear?" my dad said.

We both nodded.

Forty-Nine

Three Weeks Later...

I rose early; the aroma of freshly brewed coffee lingered in the air as I walked toward the kitchen. My mouth watered. I strolled to the far counter near the sink and placed a K-cup in the dispenser. Leaning against the counter, I watched my father read the newspaper. He hadn't shown any sign of noticing that I had entered the room, which meant something in the paper had piqued his interest.

"Good morning, Dad." I woke up feeling a lightness in my limbs, something I hadn't experienced in a long time. It had vanished the day my mom got sick. Had I finally moved on? A lot has happened this year since her death. So much had changed. I had changed.

Jim and I worked through our issues and took the next step in our relationship. He came and visited me during my healing process. I guess you can say I'm finally able to allow someone to love me. I know my mom wouldn't have left me if she had a choice. Though I will always miss her, I know she was in a better place.

“Good morning, Katherine. How did you sleep last night?”

“Great,” I lied, but I couldn’t tell him that. I didn’t want my father to feel nervous or stressed. I was afraid of being sent back. My dad had placed me in an Inpatient Care Center for the past three weeks to help with both the sleepwalking and the grief of losing my mother, which was likely why I was sleepwalking. I slept better, but sometimes, my body wouldn’t stay asleep for long periods. So, I lay in bed staring at the ceiling, letting the minutes drift away. Or I would hide under the covers, reading a book to keep my father from seeing the light on in my room. I didn’t enjoy taking the pills the doctor prescribed to help me sleep because they made my head feel fuzzy. Instead, I’d wait until I was exhausted enough to sleep, which sometimes took hours. But as far as I knew, I was no longer sleepwalking.

“Are you certain you’re ready to return? Your teachers mentioned that you’re excelling in the online courses. Remember, you can always continue them from home if it becomes overwhelming for you.”

“No, I need this. Besides, I can’t live inside for the rest of my life. I have to get back out there, Dad.”

"I know, I know. I just worry. Isn't it okay for me to worry about you?"

"Don't you think you've done enough of that? I need to take care of this."

"Alright, at least sit down and have some breakfast before you leave." He pulled out the chair next to him.

Coffee in hand, I ambled over, dropped my backpack on the floor, and sat down. My eyes scanned the table, landing on the newspaper next to my dad. It felt like déjà vu from a month ago when I had seen the article about the girl found dead in the woods. The dead girl— I wasn't sure if I had killed her, but this time the article was about a boy. I shook my head. No, I had nothing to do with whatever happened to him; I was sure of it. My curiosity got the best of me, and I grabbed the paper.

"Katherine don't!" my father shouted.

What didn't he want me to see? I held the paper away from him and skimmed the words. What had happened to the boy? The boy I knew. Someone I went to school with. Someone who could've ruined my life or, worse, my father's life if he had gone to the police. If he had remembered what happened that night in the woods.

Gavin was dead.

Local Boy Found Dead:

Crawford teenager was reported dead at the scene. According to local police, 17-year-old Gavin Bowers was found unresponsive at his home. The cause of death has been ruled a suicide. Officials have not yet released information about the condition of the body out of respect for the family.

Office Wallace stated that the mother of the boy found her son when she went into his room the following morning.

"He hadn't come downstairs for breakfast, so I went up to check on him," the mother said. "Gavin was always an early riser."

Dispatch reported that the mother called 9-1-1 immediately after finding her son. According to the coroner's report, the time of death was sometime after midnight. No note was found at the scene by the deceased as to why he had taken his own life.

The Bowers family appreciates the support they have been receiving and asks that you respect their privacy.

I swallowed as bile rose in the back of my throat. My fingers went limp, and the newspaper fluttered to the floor. I turned to face my dad.

"Oh, my God!"

My dad put a hand on my arm. "Are you okay?"

"Why? Do you think he remembered what happened that night?"

"I honestly don't know, Katherine. I'm really at a loss."

I knew this was a good thing. Not that he had killed himself, but that he wouldn't be able to tell anyone about what he had seen that night. Jim was the only one who knew besides us, and he swore he would never say a word. I wasn't a killer. It was an involuntary act I had no control over. I didn't know I was doing those things, but we still had no solid proof that I had killed the girl. Now that Gavin was dead, we will never know what he did with the knife.

I bent over to pick up the pages from the newspaper when my eyes caught the words, **"Teen Arrested for Killing Girl."** I set the paper on the table and traced the article with my finger as I read it on the second page.

New evidence has surfaced in the brutal murder of a local girl, Paige Ziel, 17, who was found at Camp Wilson, one month earlier. The police fingerprinted the scene but found no match until two days ago when the mother of the recently deceased, Gavin Bowers, brought in a knife with blood on it. A knife she said she found hidden in her son's closet.

The knife was in a zip-locked bag and later processed. The police were able to lift prints from the weapon. According to the forensic report, the prints pulled from the knife belonged to Nick Miller, 19, from Carey, Ohio.

There were also two different blood samples found on the knife. One matching the girl found in the woods near Lemmon's Park back in August of this year. The family wishes not to reveal her name at this time.

The second set of blood found on the weapon belongs to an unknown person. Officials are still searching for the victim. The police were able to apprehend Miller, who was later arrested.

"According to a neighbor of the Miller's, it is very possible Nick Miller killed his parents. The neighbor went into the Miller's house to check on them and found Mr. and Mrs. Miller in their basement gagged and tied. The victims were badly beaten, with multiple blows to the head. The weapon, a baseball bat, was found near the bodies. DNA is being run on the weapon found at the scene. We believe Miller then made his way to the town of Crawford," the local sheriff stated.

"After doing a thorough investigation, the suspect in custody has admitted that he had been living in a house on Gill Road. Officials went to the house and found the body of the owner, Clare Banning. According to the suspect, he said he broke into her home, brutally raped and killed Ms.

Banning using a knife from her kitchen. The same knife was used in the Lemmon's Park murder. Miller said he placed Ms. Banning inside a large freezer in the basement of her home. The suspect has admitted to killing the girl in Lemmon's Park.

Miller also stated he had been living in a cabin at Camp Wilson, where they found the body of Paige Ziel. This is an ongoing investigation as more information and evidence is being processed."

I gasped when my eyes landed on the photo of Nick Miller. It was the same guy who had bumped into me on the first day of school and had stopped me in the hall. Nausea surged in the pit of my stomach as I remembered the events of that day and the thought of him being good-looking. He was a monster who raped and murdered women.

"Katherine, what is it?" my father asked.

It all made sense now as the pieces to the puzzle came together. I recalled the day after my dad was hit over the head and the blood on the floor I had scraped into a bag. I wondered if this Nick guy was the one who broke into our house, too. Had he also placed the camera on the deck? Had he been watching me the entire time? I shivered, recalling the moments when I was walking home and felt like someone was following me.

The paper left my hand as my dad grabbed it. “Do you know this kid?”

I shook my head. “I only met him a few times on the first day of school. I thought he was just another new kid.”

“Do you think he broke into our house?”

I shrugged my shoulders. “Could have been, I guess.” It made sense.

“Well, when I get to the station, I’ll speak with the Captain.”

“Here,” I said. “Take this with you.” I dashed to my room and returned with the Ziplock bag containing the blood. “Run this for DNA.”

My dad searched my face for answers.

“I found the blood on the floor, away from where you were attacked. I collected it and had forgotten about it until now.

Fifty

Five days later, the results from the swab revealed a match to Nick Miller. He had indeed been in our house, probably on his way to my bedroom, unaware that my dad was in the living room. I assumed that Nick hit my dad in the head, knocking him out. Then I came out of my room, and Eva ran after him, chasing him out the door into the backyard. Was he going to kill me like he did the others? I didn't know, but I had to find out.

Visiting the jail wasn't at the top of my list, but I needed to understand why he had been in our home. So, for the first time in my life, I skipped school and drove to the town of Carey, where Nick Miller was being held. It wasn't far—maybe an hour and a half at most. My father didn't know I was going, but I did bring Jim with me. He stayed in the car while I went inside. I had to handle this on my own.

I scanned the room with my eyes until they rested on Nick, who smiled back at me through the glass partition that separated the visitors from the prisoners. My stomach tightened. I swallowed, pulled out the chair in front of him, and lifted the phone to my ear.

"Well, what a surprise! I never thought you'd come to see me," Nick said through the phone.

"That makes two of us, but I need to ask you something."

"And what's that?"

"Why were you in my house? Why did you attempt to kill my father?"

"You truly are clueless, aren't you?"

I stared back at him. *Did I already know?* "Why don't you tell me?" I growled. He was pushing my buttons and making me angry.

"Just like I went after the other girls, you were simply another notch on my belt," he laughed. "But as usual, your daddy saved the day."

My mind flashed back to a message I had received from an unknown number. Could it have been Nick who sent it? But how did he get my number? "Did you send me a text saying, 'Your daddy won't be able to save you this time?' and 'What happened has nothing to do with you'?"

Nick's forehead creased as if my question confused him, and then he answered. "I don't play effing games with people. If I want something, I go out and get it! Besides, how in the hell would I get your cell number?"

The answer clicked in my head: who had texted me since it wasn't Nick? There were only two people who had my number, which also meant one of them had left the rat in my room as well. It had to be Trevor behind the text and the rat. But how did Trevor get into our home if Nick had taken the key?

"Did you grab the key that's hidden outside on the deck?"

His shoulders slumped. "No, I didn't know there was a key. I broke in through the basement window."

Oh. "Why? Why did you follow me?"

"Kat, right? We never officially met," he bared his teeth. "I remembered seeing you somewhere before when I noticed you standing on the sidewalk at school. Then it clicked. You were there that night in the woods. The night I killed that girl, but something seemed off about you. You were standing there, staring into space." He shook his head. "I don't think you saw me, though. Then someone else showed up, so I got the hell out of there. You didn't seem to recognize me when we ran into each other. You intrigued me, so I followed you home," he smirked.

My throat tightened again. If I didn't leave soon, I was going to hurl my breakfast. He was a sick, demented asshole. Someone who didn't belong in prison. He needed a mental hospital. I was about to hang up the phone when he shouted.

"Wait!"

I put the phone back to my ear. "What?"

"I saw you in the woods that night."

"You already said that."

"No, a different night. The night I hit you on the head. I was just about to take you when your father suddenly appeared with some boy on his shoulder. He left, and then that another girl showed up."

"Paige?" I knew precisely which night he was referring to.

"Yes, sweet Paige. She saved your life. You should thank her. Oh, wait, you can't. She's dead," he laughed heartily.

I couldn't stay here another second without wanting to kill him myself. I had gotten all the answers I needed from him and had nothing more to say to this asshole. I hoped the state of Ohio would give him the death penalty. He didn't deserve to live after killing those girls, and who knew how many others were out there and haven't been found yet? I set the phone back in its cradle and stood up. He started banging on the glass and shouting, but I continued walking without looking back.

Once outside, I took a much-needed deep breath and held it before slowly releasing the air from my lungs. A gradual smile spread across my face as the stress of knowing the truth rolled off my shoulders. I still had one last thing to do:

ask Jim about the text, the rat, and the photos deleted from my phone. I strolled over to the car and climbed inside.

"Hey," Jim said, a slow smile spreading across his face.

"Hey."

"Did you get the answers you needed?"

I nodded and shared everything with him. "You never explained why Trevor was there the day we had my dad in the trunk."

"Trevor mentioned that he went there to search for Gavin."

"In the dark?"

"I asked him the same question. He told me the police had been interrogating him for the past two hours. He said Gavin was missing, and they wanted to know if he had anything to do with it."

I nodded. That was true. I had been there and heard most of what they said. "I still need to know a few things, including who is responsible."

"Alright, go ahead."

I told him about the message and the rat that was placed in my bedroom, and of course, the photos.

"Trevor sent the text and put the rat in your room, but I was the one who deleted the photos from your phone. Once I found out you were there that night, Trevor and Mia said you probably took pictures and that I was the only one who could get close enough to delete them. I'm sorry, Kat."

"If we're going to do this, Jim," I said. "Then there can't be any more secrets. If there's anything else I need to know, tell me now before we leave this parking lot."

"No more secrets, Kat. I promise you."

I leaned over and kissed him, something we've been doing a lot since getting back together. My heart swelled with happiness, a feeling I didn't think I would experience again. Now, I had one more thing to do: talk to Mia and find out what happened to her.

Fifty-One

We spent the rest of the day talking before I dropped Jim off at his house and drove home. As I stepped out of my car, I spotted Mia sitting on the steps of her front porch. There were still things I needed to know—things I was sure she wouldn't tell me, but I had to try. I slammed the car door shut and walked down the driveway.

A moment later, I found myself in front of Mia, who remained unaware of my presence. I paused for a few more seconds, then spoke. "Hey."

Mia looked up, squinting as the sun dipped lower behind the trees and houses. "Hey."

"Mind if I sit?" She scooted over, although there was plenty of room for me next to her. Well, I guess she wasn't in a chatty mood, which meant I had to do all the talking. "So, do you want to share what's been going on?"

Mia let out a sigh, her shoulders slumping beneath her burgundy sweater—a gift I had given her for Christmas many years ago. I was surprised she had kept it and hadn't tossed it in the trash. Did that mean she still had the rest of the things I gave her? The truth is, I hadn't gotten rid of anything that belonged to her, so why was I surprised? We had a great relationship in the past. Maybe we still can. Perhaps we can rebuild what we once had.

"Mia, you know you can always talk to me about anything?"

She gazed at me with her red, puffy eyes, evidence of her tears. I wrapped an arm around her and pulled her close.

"Can we go somewhere and talk?" Her voice was soft.

"Yes, of course."

Once I was in my bedroom, I closed the door, sealing us off from the rest of the world. No one was home, and no one would hear whatever she was about to tell me.

Mia's story will be told in the book

TELL NO ONE

About the Author

Donna M. Zadunajsky is an award-winning author who began her writing career with children's books before publishing her first novel, *Broken Promises*, in June 2012. Since then, she has written several more novels, along with her first novella, *HELP ME!,* which addresses the subjects of teen suicide and bullying.

To find out more about the author, go to:

www.donnazadunajsky.com

www.ingramcontent.com/pod-product-compliance
Lightning Source LLC
Chambersburg PA
CBHW010451310726
48979CB00013B/2150/J

* 9 7 8 1 9 3 8 0 3 7 8 4 9 *